OFF SIDE

TOM
PALMER

PUFFIN

PUFFIN BOOKS

Published by the Penguin Group
Penguin Books Ltd, 80 Strand, London WC2R ORL, England
Penguin Group (USA) Inc., 375 Hudson Street, New York, New York 10014, USA
Penguin Group (Canada), 90 Eglinton Avenue East, Suite 700, Toronto, Ontario, Canada M4P 2Y3
(a division of Pearson Penguin Canada Inc.)
Penguin Ireland, 25 St Stephen's Green, Dublin 2, Ireland (a division of Penguin Books Ltd)
Penguin Group (Australia), 250 Camberwell Road, Camberwell, Victoria 3124, Australia
(a division of Pearson Australia Group Pty Ltd)
Penguin Books India Pvt Ltd, 11 Community Centre, Panchsheel Park, New Delhi – 110 017, India
Penguin Group (NZ), 67 Apollo Drive, Rosedale, North Shore 0632, New Zealand
(a division of Pearson New Zealand Ltd)
Penguin Books (South Africa) (Pty) Ltd, 24 Sturdee Avenue, Rosebank, Johannesburg 2196, South Africa

Penguin Books Ltd, Registered Offices: 80 Strand, London WC2R ORL, England

puffinbooks.com

First published 2010
006

Text copyright © Tom Palmer, 2010
All rights reserved

The moral right of the author has been asserted

Set in Sabon MT Std 12.5/17.25 pt
Typeset by Palimpsest Book Production Limited, Grangemouth, Stirlingshire
Made and printed in England by Clays Ltd, St Ives plc

British Library Cataloguing in Publication Data
A CIP catalogue record for this book is available from the British Library

ISBN: 978-0-141-32942-0

www.greenpenguin.co.uk

MIX
Paper from
responsible sources
FSC
www.fsc.org   FSC™ C018179

Penguin Books is committed to a sustainable
future for our business, our readers and our planet.
This book is made from Forest Stewardship
Council™ certified paper.

For Rebecca

CONTENTS

SATURDAY

PITCH INVASION

It was half-time in the City versus United game. Nil–nil. Sitting in the stands, Danny was waiting for the usual kind of thing that happens at every football stadium the length of England.

Garish adverts for club merchandise.

The offer of a City credit card.

Announcements about an expensive dinner where you can meet City stars from the past.

All coming over the tannoy. All at deafening volume, so it was impossible to have a conversation.

But today, for once, half-time was different.

Dad picked up on it immediately.

'What's going on, Danny?'

A group of fans were clambering over the advertising boards and on to the pitch. And a strange silence had fallen across the stadium.

'I'm not sure,' Danny said. 'A pitch invasion?'

'Hooligans?' Dad suggested.

'No. It's not like that,' Danny said.

'A protest?'

'Maybe. There's about twenty of them. And they've got . . . they've got a banner.'

3

'What does it say?' Dad asked.

Danny couldn't read it yet. He waited as the pitch invaders unfurled it. He wanted to be the first to see the banner, so he could tell his dad what it said.

Danny and his dad came to every City home game. And Danny acted as commentator because, when he was younger, his dad had been blinded in an accident. He'd had to stop work, stop playing football with Danny, stop almost everything.

Danny remembered worrying if his dad would give up *going* to the football too. But on the day of the first game after he was out of hospital, Dad had stood up.

'Danny?'

'Yeah.'

'Come on, son. City are at home. What are you waiting for?'

Since then Danny had become skilled at describing live football, telling his dad just enough so that he could follow the game.

But things were different today. Normally Danny described goals, fouls and diving continentals. Never crowd trouble. Never pitch invasions.

'They've unfurled the banner now,' he told his

dad. 'And the rest of the fans are sitting in the centre circle.'

'What does the banner say?'

'Just a minute. I can't see it.'

Two men and two women were holding the banner, turning it in a wide circle so that the fans in every stand could see it. And the TV cameras. As they did this, the crowd noise started up again. It grew louder and louder. Individual cheers and shouts merged into an increasing roar. And dozens more people ran on to the pitch to sit with the protesting fans, forcing the stewards to retreat.

'"No foreign investors for City",' Danny read above the noise.

'Ah,' Dad said. And, as he did, a chant went up around the stadium.

> *City till I die*
> *I'll be City till I die*
> *I know I am*
> *I'm sure I am*
> *I'm City till I die.*

Danny was on his feet, singing along, itching to get on to the pitch too. He had never seen anything like this at City. And he had seen a lot.

In nine years he'd been over three hundred times

since his first game in League One. He'd been five years old then. Now he was fourteen and City were one of the best teams in England. And Europe.

And it was *because* of their success that a group of money men from abroad wanted to buy the club. It was happening in a lot of places. Foreign owners coming in, trying to make money out of football clubs, risking everything the real fans cared about. The real fans knew that their club was for them. That it was about football. Not making money for people who'd never seen the team play.

That was what the protest was about.

Danny looked at his dad, who was smiling.

'What are you smiling about?' Danny asked.

'You?'

'What?'

'Dying to get on the pitch.'

'Come on, then,' Danny said, half joking, half serious.

'Me? It'd not be safe, Danny.'

Danny shrugged and watched more people running freely on to the pitch. It was a peaceful protest. The police were letting the fans make their point.

'Is it safe for you?' Dad asked.

'What?'

'If you went on, would you be safe?'

'Yes,' Danny said. 'There's loads on now. The police are just letting them do it.'

'Go on then,' Dad said, standing. 'Do it for me.'

Danny grabbed his dad and hugged him. Then he walked down the aisle and jumped over an advertising panel.

Now he was on the pitch.

And he ran. Over the touchline. Across the perfect pitch, soft under his feet. Towards the middle – and the banner. He'd never seen the stadium like this before: from the pitch. It was huge. There were other fans alongside him, waving their scarves. He lifted his scarf above his head and trailed it behind him. He looked around him. Everyone was grinning.

And he couldn't stop laughing. The feeling was amazing. He felt like he was flying. Here they were on the grass where the players ran and kicked and dived and scored.

And they were all singing: *City till I die.*

Danny sang so loud his throat ached and he knew he would lose his voice the next day. But this was important. He was a City fan. He loved the club. And, like the rest of the hundreds of fans on the pitch, he wanted it to *stay* his club. If anyone should own the club it was them: the fans.

*

7

After five minutes of protesting the fans left the pitch. Peacefully.

And the match could start again.

The second half was fantastic. The fans' passionate reaction to the foreign takeover spilled on to the pitch. What had been a tight and tense goalless match against United was now an end-to-end thriller.

City poured players forward. Their twin strike force looked lethal. Sam Roberts, England's leading scorer, and new sensation, Ghanaian international Anthony Owusu. Danny struggled to keep up his commentary just as much as the United defenders struggled to keep up with City's strikers.

'Owusu is playing deep,' Danny told his dad. 'Roberts further up.'

And as he spoke, City's midfield dynamo launched a high cross into the United area. The ball ricocheted off a defender to Owusu, who controlled it on his knee and volleyed it with amazing power. At first the ball seemed to be going way over, but then it began to dip in a powerful arc. Half a second later it was crashing in off the crossbar and bouncing about the goal.

One–nil. An awesome strike.

Danny and his dad leapt into each other's arms as the crowd exploded. First with the loudest cheer of the season, then with the name of the scorer. Over and over again.

Ow-usu! Ow-usu! Ow-usu!

When the fans had gone quiet enough for anyone to talk, Dad spoke.

'What happened?'

This always amused Danny. His dad would be leaping around, punching the air, screaming at the top of his voice one minute, then calmly asking to know why he'd been jumping around in the first place.

'Owusu . . .' Danny said breathlessly.

'I gathered that.'

'. . . he just blasted it in!'

'Yeah?'

Danny knew his dad needed more. So he decided to give it to him: like a proper reporter on the radio. He breathed in and began.

'City's amazing Ghanaian international has scored the goal of the season. Picking it up on the edge of the area, he took it on his knee, then fired an unstoppable volley past the paralysed United keeper. That's Owusu's twentieth goal of the season. And just goes to show that he deserved the African Player of the Year award he received only two weeks ago.'

But, as Danny delivered his commentary, his

mind was drifting elsewhere already. He was thinking about the City takeover bid and what – other than invading the pitch at half-time – he could possibly do to stop it.

THREE THOUSAND MILES SOUTH

The weather was cool in Kumasi, Ghana's second city. Heavy clouds seemed to be pulling the vast sky down to the ground. A breeze was making the trees and the corn fields dance.

In a clearing, on a patch of sparsely grassed land on the outskirts of Kumasi, a football pitch had been marked out and there were nets in both goals. It was one of the top places to play football in the city and the best unsigned players came here to show off their skills.

Dozens of them came every day. Game after game. It was an unofficial football academy, a place where boys with big dreams showed what they could do. And every player knew that eyes were watching: eyes that could change their lives forever.

Kofi Danquah, a sixteen-year-old boy, was on the ball now. Kofi travelled to Kumasi every day by foot or on the back of a pick-up truck. He lived several kilometres away, with his parents, who were cocoa bean farmers.

In the last year, two boys that Kofi knew had

been spotted here, then taken on to Europe to play football. One – Nelson Otoo – who was two years older than Kofi, had signed for a club in Belgium. They had seen his picture in a newspaper that the player had sent home to his family. Otoo's family were now rich. They had moved away from their old home to a wealthy part of Kumasi. Otoo's money meant that his family's life had changed forever. And not just his mother and father, but his uncles and aunts and dozens of cousins.

Other boys had gone on to Italy, France and Germany. All hoping to be the next Michael Essien. Or Anthony Owusu. To be a famous footballer.

Some had never been seen back in Kumasi again. Or heard of by their families.

Kofi always swore that if he made it to Europe he would honour his family. Like Nelson Otoo. Like Anthony Owusu.

Kofi looked up to see a pair of defenders approaching him. The one on the left was not so good. Kofi knew he could beat him easily. The one on the right, however, was Enoch Ngugi, the best footballer on the pitch. Ngugi was so good he had European clubs after him. It was rumoured that an AC Milan scout was on the touchline watching Ngugi now. All the players had noticed the two white men sitting in plastic chairs, occasionally talking to each other.

That was why this next move was so important to Kofi. If he was ever going to be good enough to have an agent from Europe take an interest in him too, he would have to be able to get past players like Enoch Ngugi.

Kofi stood on the ball and waited as the defenders came closer. Then he feinted to go right and saw the lesser defender lunge at him. Kofi took the ball past him with ease.

Now he had to beat Ngugi.

But Ngugi was strong, his bigger frame next to Kofi.

Kofi was small for his age, it was true. But he was also fast. Really fast.

So he forced himself on, trying to edge ahead of Ngugi. For a moment they were shoulder to shoulder, Kofi trying to cope with Ngugi's strength, Ngugi with Kofi's speed. Kofi knew what he had to do: he had to believe he could win this battle. *I can beat him*, he said to himself.

Then, suddenly, Ngugi was somewhere behind. Kofi *had* beaten him.

Now he was one-on-one with the keeper. This was his chance. He could feel the adrenalin coursing through him.

And Kofi thought, *What would Anthony Owusu do now?* Ghana's greatest-ever footballer. Kofi's hero. A millionaire living in England. The man whose shirt Kofi was wearing.

He'd shoot.

Kofi drew back his right leg and fired.

The ball flew like a rocket. Through the flailing arms of the keeper.

Goal!

Then the ball carried on. Through a gap in the net. Past the small crowd of men watching behind it. Eventually coming to rest at the feet of the two white men who were sitting down. One of them stood, trapped the ball and played it skilfully back towards the pitch.

But Kofi had no time to think about the white man. He was jumped on by his friends Ekow and John, who pulled him to the ground.

'Owusu,' John said. 'You're Anthony Owusu!'

After the game Kofi sat at the side of the pitch to drink water with Ekow and John. They were all thirsty and hot. It had not started raining, but it still looked like it might.

Kofi got out a needle and some thread as they talked. His Nike boot was falling apart again. He had a Nike on his left foot, an Adidas on his right.

He would normally sew it at home in the evening, but today it needed urgent attention. He focused on his job, while listening to his friends.

'Look,' Ekow said, 'Enoch is talking to a man.'

Kofi looked up. A tall black man in a wide-brimmed hat was shaking Ngugi's hand, smiling broadly.

'Do you think he is an agent or a scout?' Kofi asked, looking at John.

John shrugged. 'I do not know.'

All three boys went quiet. If Ngugi was talking to an agent, what would the agent be saying? Would he be offering Ngugi a place at a football club in Europe? Was his life about to change forever?

Kofi hoped so. He liked Enoch Ngugi. And he liked to see boys from this academy make it. It gave him hope that the same would happen to him one day.

'Excuse me?'

The voice came from behind them. It was not a Ghanaian voice.

The three boys turned to see a man. The white man who had trapped the ball when Kofi had scored his wonder goal. He was tall and athletic-looking for an older man. He looked about the same age as Arsène Wenger, the Arsenal manager. He had a wide smile of gleaming white teeth.

The man held out his hand to Kofi. After hesitating, Kofi held out his hand too. They shook.

'I'm sorry for interrupting you,' the man said. His accent was English, or maybe South African. 'I'm Jonathan Shearer. A football agent.'

Kofi, Ekow and John froze, staring at the man. They said nothing.

'I represent an English football team, City FC.'

Still no words came from Kofi. His heart was beating fast. He glanced at his friends, who were both staring at his hand. It was only then that Kofi realized his hand was still in the grip of Jonathan Shearer.

'I would like to take you to England. To play for City FC. Now, are you sixteen?' Shearer said, looking down at Kofi.

And Kofi nodded. 'Yes,' he said. 'Yes, I am.'

SUNDAY

BANK ROBBER

'But I want to go OUT!'

Danny's older sister, Emily, was shouting. Loudly.

Danny watched over the top of the crime section of the newspaper that he was reading. The whole family was sitting at the kitchen table, eating breakfast. He decided not to say anything. It was best to keep out of arguments involving Emily. And anyway his throat was so sore, he could barely speak.

'It's not fair,' Emily went on. 'All my mates are going to the festival. Everyone's going. Except me.'

'We told you about this day weeks ago,' Mum said. 'Your Aunty Vicky is coming round. *With* the kids.'

Dad was keeping quiet.

Danny had noticed this recently. It was like his mum and dad barely spoke to each other. Apart from when they were disagreeing. Like last night, when his mum had gone mad when she heard that Danny had run on to the pitch at the football. *With* his dad's blessing.

'Exactly – the kids!' Emily shouted, interrupting

his thoughts. 'Her three and Danny. They're all *kids*. But I'm not.'

'You're a part of this family, Emily,' Mum said, 'and I want you here. No argument. Now, I'm going to catch up on some work. I'll be down when Vicky gets here. OK?'

Danny's sister was seventeen. She was tall and had recently dyed her hair blonde. All Danny's mates fancied her, which annoyed him hugely.

But there was *something* in what she was saying. Danny would have liked the day to himself too. He wanted to get online and read some of the newspapers. A footballer had been burgled while he was playing in a game the day before. A City player. Danny wanted to know everything about it, then get down to the player's house to see what he could see. Just a bit of light reconnaissance.

Danny normally spent some of the weekends alone, trying to solve crimes. He'd been doing it for a year or so. He gathered evidence by reading the newspapers, by going to places where crimes had been committed and by thinking. His bedroom was more like a detective's office, with maps on the wall indicating crime scenes in the city. He also had a desk with a secret drawer and a swivel chair.

This all came from his dad, who loved detective books. Danny read the books to him. And the more

Danny read, the more he wanted to be a detective himself. In fact it was starting to happen for real. In the past six months he had helped solve two huge football crimes. The kidnap of a footballer. And even a plot to murder England players.

Danny could hardly believe it had happened when he remembered it. But it had. Danny moved on to an article about a bank robbery, but kept an eye on his sister, wondering what would happen next. As he did, she looked straight at him.

So he smiled.

She scowled back immediately.

'What are you looking at?' she barked.

'After your performance this week, Emily,' Dad said, drawing the fire away from her brother, 'I think you should be doing what you're told.'

It had been a bad week for Emily. She'd been in trouble at school *and* had come home late from a party last night.

Danny glanced at the sport section of the newspaper. He looked at the cover photo of Anthony Owusu volleying the ball into the back of the United net. City were level on points with United in second place now. Things were good.

But Danny had already read the sport. What he really wanted to know about was the bank robbery. There'd been an armed raid in the north of the city earlier in the week. At first the police had said it was a well-organized gang, because it had been carried out so professionally. But the day before they'd caught the robber: a seventeen-year-old boy from a well-off family. A boy who went to his school.

He shuffled on his chair to get comfortable, accidentally dropping the newspaper.

'What does it say about the match?' Dad asked, hearing him.

'I'm reading about that bank robbery,' he replied.

'Right,' Dad said.

'It was a lad. Seventeen.'

Suddenly the newspaper was snatched from Danny's hands. Emily. He'd not realized she was standing over him.

'That's Ben's house,' she said. 'Was it Ben?'

'Read it yourself,' Danny said.

'Just tell me,' Emily spat.

Danny paused. *Be calm*, he told himself. *Don't rise to it.*

'It *was* Ben,' he said. 'They arrested him last night.'

'Cooooool,' Emily said. 'I know a bank robber.'

'Cool?' Dad interrupted.

'Yeah,' Emily said. 'It *is* cool.'

'What's cool about getting arrested?'

'It just is,' she replied.

Danny saw Dad shake his head. 'Emily, getting arrested is serious. It could destroy his life. Especially if he has to go to a young offenders' place. It's not cool. It's appalling.'

Emily shrugged as Dad stood up to carry a couple of mugs into the kitchen. Danny could tell he was furious.

And he did agree with his dad. But he was interested in the story. Interested in Ben McNab. They had a picture of his house. A posh house. Danny was fascinated. He wanted to know why: why would a boy who had everything rob a bank?

'Do you see him?' Danny asked, wanting to know more, and feeling safe now they were alone in the sitting room.

'What?' Emily said sharply.

'Do you see Ben McNab? Do you know him now?'

'No,' Emily said. 'Well, sometimes. Why? Do you fancy him?'

'What?' Danny said.

'Nothing,' Emily went on. 'Because I know it's girls *you* like, isn't it?'

Danny said nothing. Agreeing would only lead to some other remark. But Emily was on a roll now. Somehow she'd changed the subject and the focus of her subject was making Danny feel very uncomfortable.

'How is little Charlotte?' Emily asked.

'Fine,' Danny said.

'Have you . . . you know?' Emily asked.

'What?'

Danny could feel himself blush. He remembered he should never find himself alone with his sister.

'You know . . . kissed her?'

Danny stood up. His sister was annoying. But when she got on to this it was too much.

'We're friends. Me, Charlotte and Paul. That's it.'

And it was true. Danny knew Charlotte from school. That was it. Emily was always trying to wind him up about her, making out there was more to their friendship, whether he wanted there to be or not.

'But you fancy her, don't you?'

Danny snatched the paper back off Emily and left the room. He went to sit at the foot of the stairs, glaring at the words, but not taking them in. His head was hot with anger. He hated his sister when she was in one of these moods. Sometimes she was OK. Like when he was in Moscow a couple of months before. She'd phoned him. Sounded like she missed him. But now, because she had to stay in and be with the family, Emily was like a caged animal picking on all the other animals in there with her.

Danny tried to read. Reading calmed his mind. Normally.

But this time it made him feel worse. On the inside page at the back there was a massive article about City. And the takeover that he so dreaded.

The headline was sickening.

MYSTERY FOREIGN OWNERS CLOSE IN ON CITY

It was happening – the foreign investors almost had their prize: Danny's team.

Some said that the investors were American. Like at Man U and Liverpool. But other rumours were that it was Russian money, which sent a shiver down Danny's spine.

Danny read on. The article talked about the protest at City the day before. It showed photos of the hundreds of men and women who had invaded the pitch. Danny recognized a couple of them. He'd seen them at the match. But he didn't see himself. The club, he read, had announced that supporters invading the pitch from now on would be banned from the stadium for life.

This made Danny furious. All they had been

doing was trying to make their feelings known. They were as much a part of the club as the owner. Even as much as the players. Why were the fans never listened to in football?

He decided he was going to write a letter to the newspaper. Start a campaign to stop the takeover. Try and get the club's 50,000 fans to own it together, instead of someone who didn't care about City. Like Barcelona. They were owned by over 100,000 fans who voted on who the chairman should be. That's how City should be run. Not by some far-off foreigner who cared only about making money out of a club he'd never been to.

Could that really happen? he wondered.

Danny knew a journalist on the paper well. Anton Holt. They'd both been involved in the football crimes Danny had helped solve. Holt listened to him. Holt would help.

He'd email him today. Something had to be done.

GOING TO ENGLAND

Kofi ran through the outskirts of Kumasi. It was several kilometres, but he was fit. Fit from football. Fit from working on his parents' cocoa bean farm since he could walk.

He dodged traders as he ran. The streets, as usual, were packed. Packed with people selling nuts and motorbike parts and cloth, among other things, earning money from anything they could get their hands on. This was how many people lived in Kumasi. Those who were not lucky enough to have their own small farms further out in the countryside, like Kofi's family.

And he was bursting to tell his parents his news. That he had been spotted by a football club in Europe. That all their dreams could come true.

Once he was out on the main road, he kept watch over his shoulder for a pick-up truck with space on board. Maybe he'd see someone from his village.

And within minutes he was lucky. A pick-up slowed to manoeuvre round a huge pothole in the road. Kofi waved and it stopped for him to jump on. Two pairs of men's arms came out to haul him aboard. Now he would be home far quicker. And with the breath to tell his parents his news.

As the pick-up made its way north he told the men around him about Jonathan Shearer and City FC. He was clapped on the back and given water. He already felt like he was famous.

Kofi went to see his father first. He knew he would still be on the farm and he knew – by the smell as he approached – that his father was burning off some land, to prepare it for the next growing season.

He walked along the side of a field that was on fire. The ground was hot under his bare feet. He could feel the black ash of incinerated blades of grass and plants turn to dust as he walked. The heat on his right cheek was intense.

So he darted to his left. Through the trees that were heavy with cocoa pods. To the farm. To his father.

As he walked, he ripped off any diseased pods. So the disease would not spread to the rest of the crop.

When Kofi told him his news, his father dropped everything and threw his arms around his son, then led him back to the main road, to their village. Kofi had never seen his father grin so broadly.

*

But even before they were home, news had spread to his district that Kofi Danquah had been signed by an English Premier League football team.

He and his father ran into their two-room home, where his mother was sitting at the main table. As he entered, she leapt up and held him.

Kofi was not surprised that she already knew. When other boys had been signed, the news had been round the district in minutes. There was no greater news than a boy going to play for a European football team.

Kofi was not only going to be rich himself, but now he could support his family for the rest of their lives. And not just his mother and father. But his uncles and aunts. And many others.

'What is going to happen?' Kofi's mother asked.

'He is coming here,' Kofi said.

'Who?' Kofi's mother looked alarmed.

'Jonathan Shearer,' Kofi answered. 'The man from City FC.'

His mother moved forward, knocking a stool over.

An hour later, Jonathan Shearer swept into Kofi's family's home. He looked even more impressive now. He was still wearing his expensive suit. And a tie that seemed to be threaded with gold.

Kofi watched his father. He knew he would be anxious to be a good host, to look after their guest. He also knew that his father would want to speak to Jonathan Shearer alone.

His father always did this when talking about important family business. And this certainly *was* important family business.

Kofi sat with his mother and brothers outside as his father talked to Shearer inside their home. None of them spoke. There was nothing to say. They held their breath in case they could hear a word of what was being said.

After Jonathan Shearer had shaken hands with Kofi's father and left, his father refused to speak for a minute. The whole family was watching him. Waiting to hear what he would say. What had been decided.

Eventually he spoke.

'We must find money,' he said. 'This agent needs a fee. To make it happen.'

'How much?' Kofi's mother asked, talking now in Twi, not English.

'Ten thousand cedi,' Kofi's father replied, also in Twi.

'Ten thousand?' Kofi's mother's voice sounded as if it had broken. This was more than five thousand pounds in the UK.

'Small compared to the money Kofi will be sending home each week,' his father said. 'We must sell the house or the farm or we will always regret it. What do we make from the farm anyway?' he asked. 'We work ourselves to death and are cheated at the scales. We get nothing compared to what we should get. This is our chance to escape. To build something new.'

Kofi's mother nodded without speaking.

Kofi considered what his father was saying. It was true that they worked hard on the farm. And that they were cheated out of money by the men who came to weigh and buy the cocoa beans. It was wrong.

And at that moment Kofi realized the enormity of what was about to happen to him. And to his family.

MONDAY

FAIR TRADE

Breaktime. Monday morning. And it was Danny's first chance to talk to Charlotte and Paul that week.

They met at the usual place: their *secret* place.

At one end of the school there was a four-flight staircase. Between lessons it filled with students going from English to maths, drama to science. But at breaks and dinnertime it was quiet. Empty. So nobody would notice if you carried on going down after the ground floor to an extra set of steps that served as a fire escape.

Except Danny, Paul and Charlotte. This was where they went. So they didn't have to go outside or be moved along the corridors by teachers.

Danny was first there. Then Charlotte.

Even before she sat down Danny sensed that, today, Charlotte was unusually quiet. And not looking particularly happy either. He had wanted to talk to her about his mum and dad. How they didn't seem to be getting on. But it looked like *she* needed to talk more than he did.

'What's up?' Danny asked carefully.

'Nothing,' Charlotte said, not looking Danny in the eye.

'What's up?' Danny repeated.

Charlotte sighed. 'Nothing.'

'What's up?' Danny said, grinning.

Charlotte gazed out of the bottom doors and sighed again. Danny looked at her. Her shoulder-length hair had grown since they had become friends. Now it was curling down the back of her school uniform.

'Your sister,' she said, facing him.

Danny's heart froze. His sister?

'What about her?' he said cautiously.

'She's just funny with me, that's all.'

'Like what?'

'I dunno. She acts all nice and friendly. But . . . I'm not sure. Why is she being so nice to me? She's not supposed to be nice. She's *supposed* to be angry and rebellious.'

Danny could feel himself going tense inside. He knew what Emily was up to. She was playing games. She was always playing games. But what game was she playing now? And why with Charlotte?

'She and Mum are arguing a lot,' Danny said eventually, trying to say something that had nothing to do with him and Charlotte.

Charlotte shrugged. Then neither of them spoke for a minute.

Danny was relieved to hear Paul's footsteps on the stairs.

'Where've *you* been?' Charlotte said.

'In the library,' Paul said breathlessly. 'Online.'

Danny waited for Paul to say more. It was clear he had something to tell them.

'They reckon there's some sort of meeting going on at City today,' Paul said. 'About the takeover. But City are denying it.'

'What meeting?' Danny said quickly, standing up. He was surprised that his voice echoed loudly around the stairwell.

'Something to do with the Russians. Or whoever it is that's taking over.'

'We need to get down there,' Danny said. 'There'll be a protest.'

Danny heard Charlotte laughing.

'What?' Danny asked, irritated.

'There'll only be a protest if *you* go down there,' she said. 'Nobody else is bothered.'

'Yes, they are,' Danny shouted. His voice echoed again. So much so that Paul gave him a warning look.

'Everyone's at work or at school,' Charlotte said.

'It's Monday. There'll be no one there. Is there anyone there, Paul?'

'No,' Paul said, looking at his friend. 'No one. Not so far anyway.'

'Well, *I'm* going.'

Charlotte stood up. 'No, you're not.'

Her voice was loud. Danny was shocked.

'I am,' he said, defiant.

'You're not going, Danny. You're at school today. It's Monday. And, if you've not forgotten, you're a schoolboy.'

Charlotte's face should have been smiling, Danny thought. It normally was when she was arguing with him. But this time it wasn't. Danny felt weird. She sounded like his mum.

Danny said nothing. He'd bunked off to go down to the City Stadium before. If he went, he wasn't going to tell Charlotte. Not if she was going to be like this.

Charlotte picked up on his silence. 'You're thinking about it,' she said.

'So?'

'So promise me you're not going.'

Danny shrugged.

'Promise me, Danny.'

Charlotte *did* sound like his mum now. Why was she being like this?

He could feel her eyes on him. And Paul's. Pressure building.

'I won't go. All right?' Danny said almost automatically. Not having a clue why the conversation was going the way it was.

'Yes,' said Charlotte. She tapped him on the head with her folder. 'I'm off now. You two are only going to talk about football. And, frankly, I've got better things to do.'

Paul and Danny stood in silence, listening to Charlotte's footsteps going up the stairs.

Paul raised his eyebrows at Danny.

'What?' he said. He felt defensive. Uneasy.

'You and her,' Paul said.

'What?'

But before Paul could reply, the school bell went. He grinned at Danny. 'What have you got next?' he asked. 'History?'

'Yeah,' Danny said, relieved that Paul had obviously let him off the hook this time. 'I'll see you later.'

Paul sprinted up half the steps, then turned to look back at Danny, who was still standing there.

'You are *going* to history?'

'Course I am,' Danny said, smiling.

History this term meant slavery.

Having to be in this lesson instead of casing the City Stadium felt a bit like slavery to Danny. He was desperate not to be there.

'So who can remind us of what we covered in the last lesson?' the teacher, Mr Reynolds, asked.

No one spoke. They just stared at the display he'd made on the wall last term. For Black History Month. Pictures of boats full of black people in chains. Diagrams of how many slaves could be fitted into one ship.

'Danny?'

Danny knew that was coming. More often than not Mr Reynolds would ask *him* to recap the previous lesson. He didn't know why.

'We talked about the transatlantic slave trade, sir.'

'And what did we learn?'

'That the British bought millions of slaves from Africa, shipped them to places like America and the West Indies. And that cities like Liverpool and Bristol were built on the profits of slavery.'

'Good. And where did most of this happen in Africa?'

'The Gold Coast,' Danny replied, surprising himself.

'And why was the Gold Coast called that?'

Danny wondered why he was getting this inquisition. He wanted to think about City. Not slaves. He was sure the slaves had had a bad time, but he didn't want to worry about that now. So he decided to stop answering. Maybe Mr Reynolds would ask someone else.

'Danny?' Mr Reynolds said.

Danny sighed. He wasn't sure of this answer anyway. 'Because they paid for the slaves in gold?'

Mr Reynolds looked like he was thinking for a second. Then he smiled and said, 'No. Good try, Danny. But the answer is that it was because, before the British traded *slaves* through the Gold Coast, they traded *gold*. Like further west they traded ivory.'

Danny had switched off. He was looking out of the window.

'You've heard of Didier Drogba?' Mr Reynolds asked.

Danny suddenly snapped to. 'Yes,' he said, uncertain what the teacher was up to.

'Well, he was from the *Ivory* Coast – before he was raised in France: the coast where they traded ivory.'

Danny wondered if Mr Reynolds was doing this on purpose, talking about football. To get his attention. Whatever. Now he was certain that once this class was over he was going. To City. To see what on earth was going on.

CAUGHT IN THE ACT

Danny had been here before: a Portakabin yard next to the City Stadium.

Six months ago he'd ended up here hiding from a burglar he'd been filming. That time it'd been late at night and he'd ended up witnessing the kidnap of his favourite footballer, Sam Roberts. A footballer he'd helped to rescue. It had been his first real case as an unofficial private investigator. And nearly his last. The kidnappers had not been impressed by the successful start to Danny's career in solving football crime.

This time it was broad daylight. So he'd had to be careful, squeezing through the fence, then finding a gap between two Portakabins from where he could watch the City Stadium entrances. But he was confident that he had made it without being seen.

Danny's plan was to just sit and watch. Most people thought that detectives chased around and got into fights on a daily basis. But Danny knew better. He'd read too many mystery stories. They sat. They watched. And often that was it.

It was 1 p.m. now. He could stay here until 5 p.m. if need be. Then he'd have to go home, or his mum and dad would be wondering where he'd got to.

Danny always had a set of things in his bag. Things to help him. Not quite gadgets – he didn't have chewing-gum that could burn through metal like Alex Rider or fancy cars like Young Bond. But he did have a small video camera, a pair of light binoculars, a notebook and a pen. That would have to do for him. He wasn't backed up by MI6 or anyone like that.

As Danny settled down, his mobile buzzed in his pocket. He fished it out and saw he'd had a text. From Charlotte.

Where r u ? C x

He wondered what he should answer.

Be honest? Say he was at the City Stadium?

Or lie?

Danny realized that he'd lied to her already. Saying he wouldn't come down to the stadium. And she knew he wasn't at school. He considered a few decent lies.

He'd had to go home to help his dad.

His grandad had had an accident.

His sister was in trouble.

That sort of thing.

But he knew he couldn't. So he texted back:

City Stadium. Sorry. D x

Then he flicked his phone shut and slipped it into his pocket. He didn't want to know Charlotte's response – he had things to get on with.

The reason he had come to the City Stadium was to watch. If the club was having secret meetings, but saying nothing to the press, then they'd be making sure no one saw people coming and going. They'd drive them through in cars with tinted windows, so the press wouldn't see who they were. And bring them in round the back.

And that's what Danny had a great view of now.

There were plenty of press reporters at the front. Before he'd come to the Portakabin yard, Danny had sussed out the front gates. Six journalists standing around. So there must be something going on. It was impossible that the press would send so many people if they didn't have inside information.

Now that he was in position, Danny tried to remember how best to stake somewhere out. The principles were: keep yourself in the shadows, wear dark clothes, don't move about. Then you wouldn't be seen. After that the key was to watch – and record – everything. Make notes. Who is going in? Who is coming out? What are they carrying? Who are they with? What do they look like?

He was good at this. He knew what he was doing.

He settled down.

Quiet.

Still.

Watching.

After half an hour he'd seen nothing. But he knew how to be patient. To wait.

He shifted his feet to get comfortable.

And then he heard something. Behind him.

As he turned to see what – or who – it was, he noticed something ahead of him too. A shape. A silhouette between the Portakabins.

His mind was filled suddenly with memories. The last time he'd hidden here. Being chased by two burglars he'd disturbed. The fear that they might get him. The fear of what they might do to him.

But this wouldn't be them. This could be anybody. People from the football club. People from the Portakabin business. Security guards.

He hadn't expected to run into trouble this quickly.

Then Danny heard a voice. Coming from the figure ahead of him.

'Excuse me, son. Can I ask what you're doing?'

Danny was faced with a policeman. And his mind went into escape mode: should he turn, stand up and get away, through the hole in the fence?

But as he turned, he heard a noise, behind him. Again. Then he saw another policeman standing *there* too.

He was trapped between two Portakabins. One policeman in front of him, one behind him. It was hopeless.

The first policeman was still looking at him. And he realized how odd he must look. Crouching here. A bag full of things. Dressed in dark clothes.

Danny didn't know what to say. He was paralysed. His heart going so fast he had to breathe deeply and slowly to control himself.

'Nothing,' he said at last.

He felt stupid as soon as he had said it.

'Nothing?' the first policeman said. 'You know you're trespassing?'

Danny thought about playing ignorant. But he knew it always looked pathetic on *The Bill* when someone who'd been caught doing something wrong pretended they didn't *know* it was wrong.

'I'm just watching,' he said. 'I'm not doing anything illegal.'

'But you know you are trespassing. And truanting, perhaps.'

Danny paused. He felt terrible. His mind was just starting to come out of shock and realize what the consequences of this situation might be. One, he might be about to be arrested. Two, he might have a police record. Three, his mum and dad, and how they would react to this.

Danny felt like his blood had turned to ice in his veins.

'Do you understand what I'm saying?' the policeman said.

Danny nodded. This was the police. You had to do what the police said.

'I'm just watching,' he said again, standing up.

'Watching what?' the policeman said, moving back a step.

Danny decided to be honest. 'The stadium.'

'The stadium?' the policeman asked. 'Why?'

'I want to know what's going on.'

'Why?'

'Because something is going on. And no one is saying what.'

The policeman nodded. 'The football club have alerted us to the fact that some people are trying to gain illegal access to the stadium,' he said. Then he added, 'I'm arresting you for trespass. You are not obliged to say anything, but anything you do say will be noted down and may be used in evidence. Do you understand?'

Danny nodded. He understood. But he didn't feel like he was there. Except that he felt sick. His mind was flitting off in a dozen directions. Charlotte. Paul. Emily. School. His dad. His mum. And how this would make them argue even more.

'Do you have anything to say?'

Danny shook his head. He could feel hot tears forming in his eyes. Because he'd just had another thought. A terrible thought. If he was being arrested, did it mean that he *would* have a police record and that now he could never be a police officer? Did it mean he could never be a real detective?

The policeman went on, reading Danny his rights.

'You will be detained to enable further investigations to be carried out regarding the offence and/or as to whether or not you should be reported. You will be taken to a police station where you will be informed of your further rights in respect of detention.'

But the words sounded distant, like they were coming from a car radio parked halfway down the street.

CAUTION

Danny waited in a small room at the police station. Alone. There were no pictures on the wall. A blind was drawn over the window in the door.

He was glad to be alone. He wanted the quiet to think clearly.

But how *could* he think clearly?

He had just been arrested. He was in a police station. In police *custody*.

And to make it worse, his mum and dad were on their way.

They would be furious with him. But Danny couldn't focus on how awful it was going to be when they got here – his mind was still trying to take in what had happened to him in the last hour.

First the police had cornered him.

Then they'd read him his rights.

Then they'd led him to a police car and, putting a hand on his head like they always did on TV, eased him into the back seat of the car. Danny couldn't resist having a look around at the car's inside. There were extra panels with buttons on. For sirens and lights, he assumed. Plus a radio and labels all over the dashboard, saying what each device was for.

In the car the police had been friendly.

It was almost – although he'd never admit it to his mum – interesting. What better way to understand police procedure than to be arrested yourself?

Danny watched as the policeman quickly keyed a four-number PIN code into one of the devices: 8254.

Danny always tried to see what PIN codes people entered. Then he remembered them. Maybe one day they'd be useful.

'What were you up to, son?' one of the policemen had said, leaning back from the passenger seat.

He had already decided to be honest when they asked questions. So he answered quickly.

'I was watching to see who was having meetings at City.'

'Yeah?' the policeman had said, sounding almost excited. 'What did you see? Anything?'

Danny saw the second policeman – who was driving – slap the shoulder of the one talking to Danny.

The first policeman had smiled. 'Not that I'm encouraging you, son,' he added.

Danny was sure the policeman was a City fan. So he took a risk. 'If someone takes over the club now, who knows what they'll do to it. But if we can just buy it – the fans – we'll be in control. That's why I was there watching.'

It was the driving policeman who spoke next.

'Well, next time watch without trespassing. Yeah?'

'I will,' Danny had said. 'I promise.'

He'd read so many crime novels by now he knew that, if arrested, you should always agree with policemen, make them feel like you really respect them. And he *did*. He loved the police. So much so that he wanted to be one.

Danny had stayed silent for a moment. He knew the driver disapproved of the other policeman being so friendly to Danny.

'So what happens now?' he'd asked.

'This is your first offence, right?' the first policeman said.

'Yes. Definitely.'

'Well, it's likely you'll get a caution. No record. Then we'll send for your mum and dad to come and get you.'

'Right,' Danny said, knowing he sounded reluctant.

'And if they've got any sense,' the driving policeman said, 'they'll ground you for the next six months, dock your pocket money and have you doing all the washing-up for a year.'

*

And now here he was, waiting in a small room, four walls, a table and three chairs.

Waiting to see how his mum and dad would react to being told that their son – who was never in trouble – had been arrested.

An hour later Danny was in the back seat of his mum's car. Heading home.

She had not spoken to him or to anyone in the police station. Dad had done all the talking to the police that needed to be done. In fact, his mum had not spoken to his dad either.

Danny expected Mum to lay into him once they were out of the building. But she'd remained silent as they walked across the car park. Then silent in the car as she drove them home.

It was a silence that was unbearable. Danny would have preferred raised voices, recriminations, shouting – anything. But all he could listen to was the changing of the gears and the car's tyres hitting potholes in the road.

Danny had decided to say nothing. Not to speak until spoken to. He closed his eyes. And kept them closed.

When they came off the main road and up Foxglove Avenue, where they lived, Danny opened his eyes. He had sensed the car slowing. The gear shifts it made as they approached their house. And he knew he was home.

What he *didn't* know was what was going to happen next.

As his mum reversed the car into the usual gap, Danny looked up at the house. At the front window. Straight into his sister's eyes.

She was laughing.

This was bad. The next few minutes, hours – maybe days – were going to be terrible.

DETECTIVE NO MORE

'Sit in there.'

Mum pointed into the front room. Her voice was ice-cold. Danny had heard her speak like this to his sister. But never him. It was a horrible feeling.

He went into the front room and sat down.

Then he waited. On the sofa, a tasselled cushion on his knee. The curtains were drawn, a table lamp lit.

His mum and dad were in the kitchen.

He tried to work out what was going on by listening. He closed his eyes to focus. But he could only hear the odd word, not full sentences.

Still, he knew they were arguing.

Arguing.

'. . . that you encourage him to do this sort of thing . . .' he heard his mum say.

'He's fourteen . . . freedom,' Dad replied.

'Does he?'

'Yes, because isn't it better he does it . . . his *life* . . . take this away from him . . .'

But Danny wasn't getting everything. Their words were broken by noises from the kitchen.

And other noises: his sister's soft footsteps coming down the stairs.

Danny swallowed. This was great. He'd been arrested and cautioned by the police. His parents were arguing because of him. He was going to get some serious punishment. And his sister was about to come into the room.

Danny breathed in. His chest ached. Could it get any worse?

'Hey, Danny Boy.'

Danny Boy wasn't good. *Danny Boy* meant Emily knew she had the upper hand.

Danny said nothing.

'What have you done?' Emily asked. She was beaming with delight.

'Nothing,' Danny said.

'I don't think so,' Emily said, her voice breaking into a laugh.

Danny shrugged. He knew what his sister was thinking. He knew she was delighted that for once it was not her who was in trouble, but Danny.

'So why are Mum and Dad arguing about you?' Emily insisted.

Danny blanked his sister. He had nothing to say to her. All she wanted to do was stir it. She didn't care about him.

Then his mum's voice, coming from the hallway. 'Upstairs, Emily.'

'But I want to watch TV,' Emily purred.

'Upstairs.'

Danny watched Emily pausing, wondering what to do. He could see her calculating.

'OK.' She shrugged. 'Call me when you're done with him.' She was beaming again.

Danny listened to her footsteps dancing up the stairs as his mum followed his dad into the sitting room. Mum shut the door behind her.

Another pause. A too-long pause. And Danny found himself craving his parents' anger.

He could see Mum looking at Dad. As if she wanted him to start telling Danny off. But he was sat stony-faced, speechless.

'What were you doing?' Mum asked, her voice surprisingly soft.

Danny had decided to be completely honest with them about what he had done. He knew – from experience – what happened when you lied. It came back to haunt you. And he wanted to get this over with.

'I was watching who was coming in and out of the stadium,' he confessed. 'To see if I could find out anything about the people who want to buy City.'

That was honest, he thought. *That was clear*.

'And you needed to truant from school, trespass on private property and get yourself arrested to do that?' Mum said, still soft. Frighteningly soft.

'I'm sorry,' Danny said. He knew that after honesty, the best thing to do was to apologize.

'So am I, Danny,' Mum said, looking at Dad. 'So am I.'

But Dad added nothing.

And Mum stood up. 'This is one of the most horrible days of my life, Danny.' Her voice was hard and strained.

Danny looked at her. Her eyes were red. She went on.

'I never thought I'd have to go and pick my son up from a police station because he had been arrested – *and* hear him cautioned.' Mum's voice was increasing in volume now. 'And then to hear you . . . to hear you explain it away like it is normal for you to get caught trespassing. Like it is normal for you to truant from school.' Mum sat down, staring fiercely out of the window. Not at him.

'It has to stop, Danny,' Dad said quietly.

'What?'

'Putting yourself in danger. Missing school. Breaking the law,' Dad said.

Danny nodded. 'OK.'

'Do you want to be a detective?' Mum interrupted sharply.

Danny wasn't sure how to answer.

Mum caught his eye. 'I mean in the future,' she said. 'When you're an adult.'

'Yes,' Danny said.

'Well, it won't happen if you get a conviction, Danny,' she said. 'You can't join the police if you have a conviction. Your life changes forever if you get a conviction. You can't go to places like America. You can't get all sorts of jobs. You're marked once you've been convicted.'

Danny nodded. 'I know,' he said.

'That's it, then,' Mum said.

Danny did not reply. He knew what was coming. His punishment. And he could see that Mum was looking at Dad again. She was going to make him deliver the final blow.

'No more, Danny,' Dad said, understanding it was his turn to speak.

'No more what?' Danny asked.

'No more of all this,' Mum interrupted. 'I want the maps down off your walls. I want the notebooks packed away. I want the desk and the swivel chair out. I want it all to stop.'

Danny's mouth went dry. He couldn't imagine

his room without his maps and notebooks. Without his detective agency.

But he'd brought it on himself. He knew that too.

And there was no arguing with Mum. Not this time.

Upstairs, Danny gently eased the pins out of his wall. His giant map of the city cracked and crumpled as he took it down. He placed everything in a box. And when it was all in the box, he closed the lid.

He felt terrible. Like he was cutting an organ out of his body and packing it away.

Once he'd finished he picked up his mobile and called Charlotte. He needed to talk to her too.

The phone rang only twice before she picked up. Danny took it as a good sign. She was going to be OK with him.

Except she hadn't picked up; she'd hung up.

He called again. Two rings. Then the busy signal again.

Danny stared at the bare walls of his bedroom. And back at his unanswered phone.

Then he closed his eyes and began to wonder: what *had* he done?

TUESDAY

LEAVING HOME

Kofi was very nervous. He had never flown in an aeroplane before.

But he had been to the local airport. Many times. He had gone there with his friends John and Ekow. Some days, when there was no football match being played, that was where they would go. It was a long walk to Kumasi, Ghana's second city, but it was always an exciting day.

They would stand at the high fences that cut off the main road from the runways. Watching as the planes moved slowly out to the tarmac. Then spellbound as they rose noisily into the sky, their propellers buzzing like giant insects.

The impossibility of it all overwhelmed Kofi. He believed in Jesus. And he had never seen Jesus. He believed that his grandfather had loved him when he was a child. And he had no memory of his grandfather.

But every time he watched the planes take off, he could not believe that such enormous machines made of metal, carrying people and their bags, were floating in the air.

Kofi had never been to *this* airport before – the international airport – where people left on long journeys or went to meet travellers they knew.

He was glad, today, the day of his first flight, that his mother's cousin Raphael was with him. Raphael had flown before. To the United States of America and back. He knew what to do at an airport. Especially this airport. There were dozens of counters and people with different faces. More white people. And Lebanese people.

Wearing his suit and carrying his briefcase, Raphael guided Kofi. He directed him to the place where he had to check in. At the desk where he had to show his passport, his flight tickets and his visa to get into England. It was here that Kofi had to hand over his suitcase. All his clothes. All his possessions. Everything. He did not know how long he would be in Europe before City FC let him return, but he did not own much anyway.

Then Raphael took him upstairs to the security barriers and told him what to expect next. An X-ray machine. A body search. Questions. Then the bright lights of a shopping area, where tourists, his cousin told him, could buy the traditional craftwork of Ghana (made in China) and bars of cocoa butter soap for the greatly over-inflated price of $7. And finally, gate two, where his plane would be flying from.

As Raphael held his hand he spoke softly to Kofi. 'We are all proud of you, Kofi. You take the hopes of the whole family with you. After all they have done for you, will you always remember to look after your parents and your family?'

Kofi nodded. He knew what Raphael was saying to him. That he must support his greater family. Those who had made sacrifices to send him to Europe. Huge sacrifices. They now depended on him to repay them with support that would help his relatives. Many families did this in West Africa: saved all their money and gave it to one member of the family, who used it to go to Europe to make more money.

And he would. He would make them all rich. He would repay them for giving him the chance to become a footballer in Europe.

As they parted on the top floor, before the security gates, Raphael gave Kofi two things: a mobile phone with a UK SIM card already installed and a large, heavy coat.

'You'll need both of these,' he said, grinning.

Once he was airside, Kofi texted Jonathan Shearer to say he was about to fly out. It was the first text he'd sent on his own phone. He'd only done it on his father's phone before. A minute later he received a text from England:

OK. C U in UK. JS

Getting on to the plane was a little like getting on a bus. Except he had to climb thirty or forty steps. Once he was on, a white woman wearing a dark blue uniform and hat looked at his boarding pass and pointed him to his seat: L10. Twelve rows up, then on the left.

Kofi had a window seat.

He had asked Raphael to try to arrange a window seat for him – and his mother's cousin had made it happen. Kofi was delighted. It meant he would be able to see the world from 30,000 feet up. It meant he would be able to trace the plane on the screen that showed a map of where they were flying. Over Ghana, its farms and forests and lakes. Such a huge scene that Kofi imagined you'd have to go up the highest mountain in the world to get such a view. A view he'd only seen in the atlas they had at the school he used to go to. Then – in seven hours – he would be in England.

What would that place be like? Would everyone be as rich as he had heard? And would they be as unfriendly as was said? He was always told that

Ghana was the friendliest country in the world, that not all places were so nice.

And would it really be so cold that he would tremble? And did it always rain? And even snow? And what was snow like?

Kofi pushed all his thoughts away. He was starting to wonder if he would be able to cope with a new continent, a new life.

HERO TO ZERO

The first thing Danny had to do on Tuesday morning was go to his head of year and tell her that he had missed school the day before.

That had been his mum's first instruction this morning.

Danny got to school early and waited outside her office. There were very few other children around in the long, overlit corridor. But those who came past looked at Danny oddly, then shuffled on.

'Hello, Danny,' Mrs Page said when she arrived, carrying a box and a stack of files. 'You're in early. What can I do for you?'

She invited him into her cluttered office and offered him a seat.

Then Danny explained. Like he'd promised he would. He'd missed school. Yesterday afternoon. He was sorry.

Mrs Page was OK with him. At first she was surprised. Then she asked him why. Why had he left school in the middle of the day? Was something troubling him? Could she help?

'It's just you've never done this before,' she said. 'You're usually such a good young man.'

Danny wondered if he should tell Mrs Page. He decided he would. She probably thought he was being bullied or something. And he didn't want her getting the wrong idea, didn't want her worrying.

'I went to the City Stadium,' he said, 'to see who was coming in and out of it. To see if I could find out anything about the people who want to buy City.'

At first Mrs Page laughed. Very briefly. Danny saw her try to control herself. Then she nodded. *Trying to look serious*, Danny thought. And that was when he saw a City mug on the sink in the corner of her office.

So *she* was a City fan too. She probably wanted to know what he'd seen. But he knew there was no way she was going to ask.

'Right,' she said, finally in control. 'Danny, this mustn't happen again. It's the first time you've done this. If you do it again you'll be on report. OK?'

Danny nodded and said thank you.

Mrs Page smiled.

And that was it.

Walking from Mrs Page's office, Danny met Paul.

'What were you doing in there?' Paul asked, nodding to their head of year's office.

Danny took Paul down the corridor to the foot of the staircase and explained. In detail. He felt safe down here. No one knew they came here.

Once he'd told his story, Paul shook his head. 'You're mad,' he said. 'Arrested? What was it like?'

'Horrible.'

'So have you got a police record?'

Danny paused before he replied. He thought he heard someone on the stairs above them. A sound, then a silence. He wasn't sure if there was someone up there. Someone listening. So he lowered his voice. He didn't want this to come out.

'No. Not unless I do something else. Then I get a police record.'

Paul shook his head again. And Danny wondered if his friend was disappointed in him. Like his mum and dad were.

But then Paul's eyes lit up. 'So, what did you see?' he said. 'At City?'

Ten minutes later Danny walked into his form room. As he did, there was a sudden cheer and round of applause. Led by James Nash.

Danny stopped in the doorway. What was going on?

Then he noticed Charlotte standing in the corner with her friends Sophie Hannah and Rachel Connor. And that she was frowning at him.

Danny mouthed, *What?* to her, but she just cast her eyes down.

Then Danny looked at James again.

'And here's the hero!' James said. 'Danny Harte. Our criminal classmate.'

The applause was louder now. Twenty faces grinning at him. Clapping and laughing.

Danny felt embarrassed. He knew what this was about. James had found out he'd been arrested. James had told everyone. James was trying to make a big deal of it. When Danny wanted to forget it.

And how had James found out? Had Paul told him? No way. He'd never do that. And he'd not had time, surely.

Danny's mind went back to when he was in the stairwell, talking to Paul, telling him what had happened. He had heard someone above on the stairs. That someone must have been James.

And now Danny wasn't sure how to respond either. How did he want to appear? What did he want people to think of him? James? Charlotte? Everyone? So – in an attempt to stop the applause more than anything else, because he'd never had attention like this before – he bowed.

'What was that about?'

Charlotte had stayed behind in the classroom, after registration. The rest of the class had gone, several slapping Danny on the back, as if to say he was cool now. Now that he'd been arrested.

'Last night . . .' Danny started to say.

'I know what happened last night, thanks to James Nash. Soon the whole school will, after that performance.' Charlotte was furious. 'You told me you wouldn't go down to City – and then you went anyway!'

Danny shrugged. He didn't know what to say. This was the first time Charlotte had told him off. If she *was* telling him off. She was really upset, he knew that. And he wasn't quite sure what to do. If his sister had a go at him like this he'd just swear at her or walk off.

But with Charlotte . . . What was he supposed to do?

'You've got nothing to say,' Charlotte said, 'have you?'

Danny desperately wanted to say something.

Should he say sorry? Should he shout back at her that he could do what he liked? That she had no right to tell him what to do?

And why was everyone on his back? He'd made one mistake and now everyone was being mean.

His mum and dad.

His sister.

And Charlotte, his . . . But that was the problem: he wasn't quite sure what Charlotte was. And she was still staring at him.

Danny felt like he was paralysed. He had nothing to say.

'You lied to me, Danny,' Charlotte said. 'That's what's annoyed me. I hate liars. That's why I like you. You tell the truth. Usually.'

Danny's head went hot. His mouth dry. His body chilled, from the shoulders down to his legs. He looked out of the window, hearing a plane descending into the airport. Then he turned to Charlotte and replied.

'So?' he said. 'You're not my mum, are you?'

After Charlotte had stormed off, giving Danny the sort of look he'd never seen her give to anyone, he had to reach out and hold one of the school tables. To steady himself.

This was terrible.

This was awful.

He wanted nothing more than to walk out of the school gates. To get away from the school, the other students and his friends.

But most of all, he wanted to get away from himself.

BAD NEWS

Kofi tried to identify every change of landscape he saw from the plane.

He recognized the edge of the Sahara Desert. Where the land changed from the lush greens and browns of Ghana to a uniform yellow. Sand. It was a dramatic difference. And it went on.

He wasn't sure, but he may have fallen asleep over the desert, because it passed quickly. Quicker than he had expected to cross what he understood was such a vast expanse.

Then he saw mountains, then sea. And then land. And he knew the land was Europe. Spain probably. The southerly tip.

He gazed down at the sea. This sea was famous. Many people in Ghana talked about passing over it. In small boats at night. To Italy. On to England or Germany. He wondered if there were any Ghanaians on the water now. Or waiting at its edge to sail tonight. Going in search of work. Of money. Of a better life. Of something to send home.

And here he was flying with a passport and a ticket to a job that would pay him more than any of those down there on the sea would earn in their lives. Put together.

That was the point in the flight when nerves began to get the better of Kofi. That was when he thought of his mother.

What would she be doing now?

Would she be making a meal for the rest of his family?

Would she be looking out towards the city? Or watching aeroplanes?

Would she be thinking about him? About how he was getting on?

And he knew what he was feeling.

Homesick.

But not just homesick. Frightened too. He was about to go to a continent that was very different from his own. Where everyone had money. Where footballers like Michael Essien and Cristiano Ronaldo walked the streets.

Then – over what Kofi thought must be France – the plane began to descend. And he knew that in less than an hour he too would be walking the streets of Europe.

Kofi was very nervous when, at the airport, he approached passport control. His mother's cousin had warned him that it would not be easy. That he must remain calm. And proud of who he was. A Ghanaian. A successful man.

'They are very careful about people coming in from Africa and other countries,' Raphael had said. 'They check your papers. They look you up on their computers. They want to make you feel that you do not belong among them.'

It was not as bad as Kofi thought it would be. He expected the police to be asking him questions. But it was just a man behind a glass screen. And he had been very polite.

'What are you coming to the country for?'

'To play football,' Kofi had said. 'For City FC.'

The man had smiled then, briefly.

'Where will you be staying?'

'With Jonathan Shearer. My agent. He is here ahead of me. Then I will buy a house to live in.'

'How long do you intend to stay?'

The questions had gone on for five minutes at most. Kofi could feel other people watching him. Some of the airport staff and passengers from the plane. He tried to feel proud, like his mother's cousin had told him to. But a part of him felt uncomfortable. To be asked so many questions. As if he didn't belong.

Out in the airport, free from any more barriers, the only strange thing for Kofi was all the white faces. Only one person in every ten was black. The rest were white. Kofi had seen white people before. But you only ever saw one or two at a time. Never hundreds of them.

It made him feel uneasy somehow. Conscious that he was black.

When they had spoken in Ghana, Jonathan Shearer told Kofi that he would meet him – with a limousine car – at the airport. To take him to a hotel suite he had booked for him. He said that Kofi should come out of the arrivals part of the airport and he would see him.

Shearer told him that he would get there in good time. That he would be sure he was not late.

But when Kofi came out of arrivals he saw no Jonathan Shearer. Only a forest of people, some holding signs with names on them: STERLAND, FAIRCLOUGH, WHITE, DORIGO.

Kofi waited next to a drinks vending machine. He noted the time: 17.54.

He looked around him, at the new world he found himself in. Apart from the white faces, he was most struck by the clothes people wore. Some were obviously very rich. Very fat. Dressed in woollen coats. But Kofi did not feel cold. It was the same temperature here as it had been in the airport in Accra and in the plane.

What else was new?

The adverts on the walls. All behind glass cases.

The covers of newspapers. Nothing like at home.

There were shops selling food and drink. McDonald's. He had heard of McDonald's, but never had their food.

Lots of colour. Lots of light.

He was taking in his new world.

Time passed.

Kofi had been trying not to look at the clock. But he couldn't help himself.

Now it was 18.21.

Where *was* Jonathan Shearer?

Kofi wondered what would happen to him if the agent never came. If he was left here in England with no ticket to go home. With no money. But he pushed the thoughts away. There was no reason to make up such terrible endings like that. Shearer had been delayed. That was all.

At 18.54 Kofi drew the mobile phone that Raphael had given him out of his pocket. He had been here an hour. He would call Jonathan Shearer. Find out what the new arrangements were.

He keyed in the number: 07375 842312. A UK number.

At first there was no sound. Then it began to ring.

Once. Twice. Three times. Then a click.

'Jonathan Shearer.' A low, confident voice.

'Mr Shearer,' Kofi said, filled with happiness to hear his agent's voice, 'it is Kofi. I am in England. Waiting at the airport.'

'Kofi?'

That was all Shearer said. Just his name. Then silence again.

'Mr Shearer?'

'Kofi?'

'Yes?'

'I have bad news.'

Kofi felt his legs go weak. As if he had just seen a snake in the grass, too late.

'City have pulled out,' Shearer said. 'I'm sorry. They no longer require a winger. You need to go home.'

'But, Mr Shearer . . .' Kofi started talking. He hoped that if he kept talking it would not be true, that he could change things. 'I am here. I have no money to go home. No ticket. I will play well for them. I will give them everything. I . . . Mr Shearer?'

The line was dead. A high-pitch squeal in Kofi's ears.

Kofi redialled. Jonathan Shearer had been cut off. He must have been about to say he had made a mistake. There was no way he would have brought Kofi to Europe unless he had a place in the City team.

But when he phoned again there was no reply. Just the high-pitch squeal again.

Kofi rang every five minutes. For an hour. Each time trying to breathe deeply. To overcome his panic.

But each time it was the same noise.

And Kofi realized that he was on his own in a strange country, with nothing.

He sat on the floor. His legs had finally gone beneath him. And although he tried to think about what was happening to him and what he should do next, he could not. His mind was frozen.

THE PORTAKABIN YARD

Tuesday, 3.30 p.m. And Danny had gone from school straight to the City Stadium.

That was where he was now. Watching.

He was not in the Portakabin yard. He'd never go there again. But there was nothing wrong in standing on the sixth floor of a storage facility, looking down through windows at the City Stadium. Over the car park. He was not trespassing here. And school was finished, so he wasn't truanting.

The storage facility was the kind of place where people with big houses and too much stuff came to put their extra things. Or – he thought – the kind of place criminals brought the things they had stolen. A safe house.

In fact, he'd read about one of these places in the newspaper recently. A local stately home had been robbed. Lots of paintings and antique furniture gone forever. Until it was found – after a tip-off – in a storage place like this.

Danny stared down at the City Stadium. He had a great view from here. He could see into the club's offices and the far corner of the pitch. He could watch the car park and the road that ran past the stadium. But – because he was further away – he couldn't see the faces of people in the car park.

And there were plenty of faces to see, dozens of people in the offices and in the car park. Danny had noticed several suited people in one of the top tiers of the stadium. He traced them as they moved about the building. Through his binoculars. Then as they emerged into the car park.

Who were they?

They could be the people who wanted to buy the club. The Russians. Danny kicked out at the wall next to him. He was furious. He needed to be closer. Then he could take photos. Put them on the City fans' website. Someone somewhere would know who they were. Then they might have a chance of stopping them.

Danny gazed at the Portakabin yard. If only he was there. He'd have head-shots of all of them. Something none of the press would be able to get. He could see them too. On the other side of the stadium. Behind a gate.

Danny's feet moved to go down the staircase.

He stopped himself.

He mustn't. He mustn't go to the Portakabin yard.

But his mind was racing. If he could get images

of the people in suits – still all standing around talking – then he could do something.

His feet moved again.

And now he was going down the stairs. Fifth floor already.

But what about Mum? If he went there how would she react? He'd made her a promise. And his dad. They'd be gutted if he let them down like this. They both thought he was at Paul's right now.

Fourth floor.

And what about his wanting to be a policeman? If he was picked up again by the police he'd have a record. Then he'd never be able to be a detective.

Third floor.

And what about Charlotte? What if he got arrested again? What would she think of him then?

Second floor.

But who was he?

If he'd already lied to Charlotte then he was a liar *already*. If he'd already let everyone down then that was who he was. Maybe he should accept it. He was a skiver, a liar, a bad son.

First floor.

What was he? Someone who always did what other people wanted, what other people expected? Or was he on his own, trying to do the right thing, even if it broke the rules?

Ground floor.

Exit.

The street.

The shadow of the stadium.

The Portakabin yard.

What was he going to do? The right thing? And the right thing by who?

STRANGE CITY

Kofi walked out of the airport to be hit by the cold air.

And that was *just* what it felt like: as if he had been struck by it.

He drew the coat that Raphael had bought for him around his chest. It was a heavy coat, feeling more like a blanket. The air was dry and, when he breathed out, it was as if smoke was coming from his mouth.

Everyone had said he would be shocked by the cold. And he was.

Shivering, he looked back through the huge glass panes of the airport at the bright lights and the shops, at the hundreds of people queuing and meeting. And at the two armed police officers who, he had thought, had been watching him.

He needed to get away from them. If they found out he had no one to meet him here, what would they do? Would they ask him all those questions again? Would he have to give different answers? And what would they do with him when they knew the truth?

Kofi wondered if they would put him on a plane, send him back to Ghana. Part of him yearned for that, to be out of this strange country, this cold world. But then another thought came to him. If he were to go home, what would his family say to him? If he told them he had taken all their money and that he had nothing to give them in return. He could not do that.

And a part of him knew the whole thing was a mistake. That everything would be OK.

So he began walking. Just walking. To look as if he was going somewhere, maybe to meet someone.

He went away from the front of the airport terminal. He was shocked that everything was so different. Not just the air, but the trees and the buildings. There were tower blocks with dozens of floors. One after the other as the road led away from the airport. And the trees were darker and taller. And they had grown in rows, like they'd been put there on purpose.

As he walked, he glanced around him. What were the threats? he wondered. Would there be gangs of children with knives, like he'd been warned? Would the police be searching for people who had come over from places like Ghana, to send them back or put them in prison?

He knew it was important that he appeared to

have a purpose. So he looked at the sign posts. CITY CENTRE, some said. That was where he would go. That was where the football stadium would be. Like in Kumasi. He would go there and ask the City FC people to take him on. Tell them that he had come this far and that it was not fair to leave him like this. He would do it first thing in the morning. He would find the coach and show him how good he was at football.

So Kofi carried on walking. Towards the city centre. Over busy roads with eight lanes of traffic. Over footbridges.

He followed the signs. Soon he could see the city's lights. Tall towers. Floor after floor of illuminated buildings. It was like Accra had looked in the dark, the night before Raphael had taken him to catch the plane.

Kofi walked along what looked like a motorway. But there were houses on each side. Large houses with grass and tall trees. Most of them had curtains drawn across the windows. At first he had walked beside the houses. But in front of a row of buildings that looked like they could be important shops, with great iron shutters outside, a large group of boys, some on bicycles, started to shout at him.

When they did, he knew to run. Without even looking back, he ran across the road as fast as he could. He could hear them laughing. Loud, raucous laughter. Within seconds the sounds had faded and he saw that they had not even tried to follow him.

The walking was helping to keep him warm. He knew that when he stopped walking he would have to find somewhere to shelter. He felt confident that he would be able to find a place to sleep. It would not be like it was in Accra, where some children slept in the street. Here the streets would be empty. There would be no night people. Here everyone had money. Everyone had a home.

Some time after he had run from the gang of boys he found himself climbing a hill. He was not used to hills. The streets rose, houses built at their sides. But soon he came to the top. He was suddenly struck by the beauty of the country he had come to. Black hills. Lines of street lights heading into the distance.

And then he saw, among it all, a black shape, unlit.

Instinctively he knew what it was. He had seen this in Kumasi. A football stadium at night. The patch of dark surrounded by street lights. Empty and quiet.

That was where Kofi would go.

He would sleep in the stadium. In one of the stands. At the side of the pitch. Then, in the morning, he would go to talk to the coach and show him what a great footballer he was.

Kofi was starting to feel better.

The football stadium was like a fortress. Huge iron gates. Walls without windows. Great sheets of glass. And three times as tall as Kumasi's stadium.

Kofi wandered to the front entrance, a huge City FC badge lit up on the wall, and came eye to eye with a man in a uniform. The man was sitting behind a desk. He stood when he saw Kofi. So Kofi waved, then jogged off.

He realized he had been stupid thinking he could sleep in the stadium. He would have to find somewhere better.

He looked around. He felt hopeless, a panic rising inside him. What would happen to him?

He kept walking. And that was how he found the warehouses. Up the road from the great football stadium. A cluster of one-storey concrete buildings. With big signs on the doors and car parks.

There was no one here.

It would do. For tonight.

MAN IN THE DARK

It was dark as Danny walked along one side of the Portakabin yard.

He was determined not to go in. However much he yearned to. If he went in there and was caught, his parents would kill him.

With no other way to go, he walked through a ginnel to what looked like a set of small industrial units. They also bordered the City Stadium's car parks. Maybe Danny could watch from here without having to trespass. There must be somewhere that wasn't private property.

Coming round the corner and into the industrial area, he was struck by a vivid memory. This car park was where his dad used to leave the car. When his dad was still able to drive to the football.

Danny stopped still for a moment. In his mind, he saw his dad reverse the car into a space among all the other cars. City stickers on windscreens. Scarves hanging out of windows. Dad making sure Danny was safe. He was young then. Six or seven. Before Dad had the accident.

Danny didn't know whether to smile or cry. He

wished he could call his dad and tell him where he was. To enjoy the memory. But he wasn't really sure that Dad would want him here, even if he wasn't doing anything wrong. Not *really* wrong.

Then he saw a gap. Between two of the industrial units. A metre or so across, it was wide enough to walk down. And it was dark, shaded from the street lights by two roofs overhead that seemed to meet above the gap.

And at the other end of the alley: a clear view of the City Stadium. And he was not trespassing.

Perfect. He could watch from here. Maybe get some photos, even though it was dark.

If he could just get some shots of people, put them up online and see if anyone knew who they were, he could start to solve this mystery.

But then something moved.

At first Danny thought it was a dog.

But this was not a dog; it was a person.

Danny stepped back.

The person had stopped moving.

What if it was a policeman?

Again.

That would be it. He'd be in so much trouble. With everyone. But a policeman would be walking *towards* Danny. This person was squatting at the end of the alley, not moving.

Danny wondered what to do.

Go away? Leave whoever it was to whatever they were doing?

Say hello? Maybe it was a journalist doing what Danny himself was planning on doing. And, if it was, that could be useful. Really useful.

Then another possibility came into his mind. Maybe someone was injured. Or in trouble.

Danny decided to say something. If he could help, he would. But what he really wanted was to see out of the end of this alley and gather information.

Danny stepped forward, letting his eyes adjust to the dark.

'Hello?' he said.

No answer.

'Hello?' Louder this time.

The figure moved, as if trying to hide.

'Can I help you?' Danny said. 'I mean, are you all right?'

The figure moved again. Rocking, it seemed. Then on his feet.

Danny saw him come closer. They could look into each other's eyes now. But neither of them spoke.

It was a boy. He was somewhere between sixteen and seventeen, black with shaved hair. He was short, a bit smaller than Danny. And his eyes were wide and full of life.

Danny stepped back. Partly to allow the boy to come out of the alley. Partly because he was afraid of what was going to happen next.

HAPPY MEAL

'Are you all right?' Danny asked again.

He could see that the boy facing him was very nervous. And Danny was well aware that he was standing in the path of his only escape route.

Then the boy spoke in a heavily accented voice. 'Are you from City FC?'

Danny smiled, but swiftly stifled it. Was he from City FC? That was his dream. He wished he could say yes. The remark disarmed him. This was no psycho waiting to attack someone. No mugger about to rob him.

'No,' Danny said carefully. 'I *support* City. I'm a City *fan*.'

He was trying to work out who the boy was. His English had an unusual accent. Danny assumed either he was from somewhere in Africa or that his parents were, remembering how footballers like Michael Essien and Lucas Radebe talked. He also noted the boy's clothes now he could see better in the dark. He was wearing a huge coat, like something you'd see in a fifties film, but the clothes looked different, not what you'd expect an English sixteen- or seventeen-year-old to be wearing.

'Are you from round here?' Danny said, knowing he sounded a bit ridiculous.

'No,' the boy said.

'Are you in trouble?' Danny asked.

The boy shrugged.

And Danny realized that the boy didn't trust him. He wasn't surrendering any information. He was just answering with one word – or a gesture.

Danny had to make a decision: leave him or try to help him.

'Do you want me to go?' Danny asked.

The boy paused this time. Then he shrugged again.

'Maybe I can help you,' Danny said. And he meant it. He wanted to help him.

The boy looked at him.

He's evaluating me, Danny thought. *He's working out if he can trust me. How can I make him trust me?*

'Do you want some food?' Danny asked.

The boy nodded quickly, then stopped himself.

'Do you?' Danny asked. 'If you wait here, I can get you some. Do you like McDonald's?'

The boy's eyes widened. 'I have never eaten McDonald's,' he said.

Danny nodded. 'But you eat meat?'

'Yes. Yes, I like meat.'

'Wait here,' Danny said. 'There's a McDonald's five minutes away. I'll be quarter of an hour.'

The boy nodded.

Danny smiled. Then he left the boy crouching back in the shadows. He decided that was the best thing to do. Give the boy time to gather himself. And – if Danny brought him food – win his trust.

But Danny knew there was a strong chance the boy would be long gone by the time he got back.

Danny walked quickly through the industrial estate. Then across the main road that led to the City Stadium. Two hundred metres ahead he saw the McDonald's.

As he approached its bright lights he wondered what he was doing. Why was he buying a meal for a boy he had met in between two units on an industrial estate? Wasn't he putting himself in danger? What was the right thing to do?

He wasn't sure about that. But he was sure that he needed to do this. He liked to get to the bottom of things. He liked to know what was going on.

What would his heroes do?

Recently he'd been reading books by a Swedish author called Henning Mankell to his dad. He

loved the main character, who was called Kurt
Wallander. Wallander was moody but good. He
always tried to do what he thought was right. And
that included helping people he thought were in
need of it, even if he was scared of them.

Danny decided that Wallander would help this
boy. So that was what he would do too.

Kofi sat down and waited for the white boy to
come back.

What else could he do?

He had found a good place to hide, a sheltered
place. And a white boy had come along and offered
him food. In Ghana that is what people would also
do. Share their food with a stranger who was
hungry. But he had heard that people in Europe
were not like that, that they were not so generous.
But the white boy had proved that wrong. He
wondered if all the things he had heard about
Europe before coming here were nonsense.

As Kofi waited for the white boy to come back
with his food, he realized he was hungry. Very
hungry. And cold. Ever so cold. Maybe food would
help warm him.

But then another thought came into his mind.
Maybe this was a trap. Maybe the boy had gone
away not to get food, but to get the police.

Kofi stood up. Maybe he should run again. Find somewhere better to hide than this.

When Danny came back with two Happy Meals the boy had gone. Danny was sure he was between the right units, but he decided to check the other gaps between buildings in case he'd made a mistake. It was always possible he'd made a mistake.

But the boy was not there.

What should Danny do? Maybe the boy was playing tricks on him. Maybe he'd run off. Maybe he was waiting to attack Danny. Any of these things was possible.

But something about the boy made Danny want to help him. He was sure he was scared, not hostile. He decided to go to the place he'd found the boy and wait.

Danny edged down the alley. No, the boy was not there.

Then, five minutes later, Danny heard a foot on gravel behind him. He turned. *Was* it a trap? *Was* he about to be attacked?

The boy stood in front of Danny warily.

Danny knew to stay calm. Always stay calm. Never overreact.

'Here's your food,' he said, holding out the Happy Meal.

The boy took it, then crouched down, opening the bag.

He looked up at Danny.

Danny sensed confusion.

'Each thing is wrapped,' Danny said. 'There's a burger. Some chips. Some onion rings.'

The boy grinned and nodded. 'I am Kofi,' he said.

'Danny,' Danny replied, sitting down beside him. 'That's my name.'

'Danny,' Kofi said. 'Thank you, Danny.'

The two boys sat in silence as they ate.

Danny looked over to the City Stadium. The people he had been looking for – the men in suits – would now be long gone. He'd lost any chance of finding out who they were. If they were involved in the takeover of the club.

He noticed that Kofi ate quickly. And that by the end of the meal he was grinning.

'Good?' Danny said.

Kofi nodded. He felt OK. The best he'd felt since he came to England.

Then Danny asked him, 'What's happening, then? Are you in trouble? Can I help you?'

HELPING KOFI

Kofi spoke for a long time in a quiet and slow voice, articulating what had happened to him. And telling Danny about his parents' farm and how they'd sold it to help him.

Shocked by the story he was hearing, Danny said nothing throughout. Although he had dozens of questions, he thought it best to wait until the end. He didn't know what to tell Kofi about his fantasy that tomorrow he would be able to go and talk to City's coach. That was, of course, impossible.

But he did know what the right thing to do was.

'You must come home with me. Now,' Danny said.

As soon as Danny had said it he saw Kofi go in on himself, as if the suggestion panicked him.

'What?' Danny asked.

'It is very kind of you,' Kofi said, 'but I cannot.'

'Why?'

'I must be here. But it is very kind of you. Please do not be angry that I say no.'

Danny wasn't angry. But he didn't know why Kofi was turning him down.

'Then let me help you,' Danny said.

'How?' Kofi asked. 'I know you think my idea to speak to the coach tomorrow will not work.'

Danny frowned. How did Kofi know that? Then he smiled. Kofi was no fool.

In fact, he felt that *he* was more of a fool. He wanted to help this boy – in a foreign country, his country. But he had no idea how. It was a big question.

He gazed across at the City Stadium.

And – as he did – the answer came to him.

Anton Holt.

Anton Holt was one of the UK's leading football newspaper writers. He was also someone Danny knew really well. Maybe he would know what to do.

Danny had met him six months ago when they'd both become involved in the kidnap of England's leading scorer, Sam Roberts. Between them they'd solved the crime and rescued Roberts. Then four months after that, they'd travelled to Moscow to watch England, but they became involved in stopping a crazed Russian billionaire from murdering England goalkeepers.

Holt would know what to do.

Holt could help.

'I know a journalist,' Danny said. 'A newspaper writer.'

Kofi nodded. 'Yes,' he said. 'I know what you mean.'

'He can help. He might take you to talk to City. After he has spoken to you.'

Kofi nodded again. 'Is he good?'

'Is he a good person?'

'Yes. Is he good? Like you.'

Danny smiled. Kofi had paid him the best compliment.

'Yes,' Danny said, 'he's good. He's very good.'

And Kofi nodded.

Danny took his mobile out of his pocket. He found Holt's number and called him.

But there was no ringing. Just his answering service.

Danny knew what that meant. Holt had turned his phone off. He was probably with his girlfriend. And his phone would be off all night.

Then Danny saw the time: 8 p.m. He was late.

He stood up quickly. Too quickly. Because Kofi looked panicked again.

'It's OK,' Danny said. 'He's busy. But *I'm* late. I need to go home. My parents will kill me.'

Kofi nodded. But Danny saw that he had doubt in his eyes. The kind of look he'd had before he trusted Danny.

*

Danny walked briskly out of the industrial estate, putting his hoody up. Kofi had agreed to stay where he was. And Danny had taken Kofi's mobile phone, which had run out of power. It was the same model as his sister's, so he said he'd get it charged. Then they'd be able to communicate if Danny wasn't with him.

Danny promised to get Holt's help, then return and tell Kofi everything.

As he came out on to the main road, Danny was met with flashing lights.

A police car. And it was slowing down, the door opening.

Danny didn't know what he'd done wrong – nothing as far as he was concerned – but he knew he had to get out of there. Innocent or guilty. He had too much to lose.

And he also knew that he was scared. Again.

So he did the only thing he could think to do: he ran.

THE CHASE

He ran without thinking. Across the road. Towards the football stadium.

'Hey, stop!' he heard one of the policemen shout.

What would happen to him now – if the police caught him?

He'd done nothing wrong. But, because he was running, he'd suggested he *was* doing something wrong. Even if he was just brought home by the police he'd be in severe trouble at home. And what would they do about his caution? Would they give him another? Or worse?

So he kept running. Over the road. Into the car park at the back of the chip shop, Hand of Cod.

Danny needed an alleyway. Or something that was not a road. If the police followed him on the road, in their car, they'd catch up with him in seconds.

At the back of the chip shop there was a cul-de-sac. A street of houses. Danny had walked here before. There was an alley at the end. He'd go up there.

By now he was running at top speed. He knew he was fit. He didn't smoke, like some other kids his age, so he could run with full lungs of air.

Instead of looking back to see where the police were, he just ran, not listening to hear if they were chasing him. He ran past families getting out of cars. Past men pulling shutters down in front of shops. Past queues of traffic heading home.

The air was thick with exhaust fumes.

Ten minutes later Danny felt safe. He was on the top of the hill now. There was a large grassy slope here, a playground and a row of trees. He headed left, for the trees. Towards a bench where he could sit and get his breath back.

Danny noticed that there was a group of lads his age in the playground. They appeared to be making a fire on a children's roundabout – or something like that. And they were all wearing hoodies like him. They'd already started staring at him. Like they wanted trouble.

And Danny smiled. He knew what sort of trouble they'd bring. Lots of bravado. Asking him stupid questions. Shouting stuff. But he could cope with that. It was easier than being chased by the police – and easier than coming across a strange boy hidden in an industrial estate.

Danny sat on the bench.

Think. He needed to think. About Kofi.

He decided he'd go to Anton's office first thing

in the morning. Before school. Anton got in early. Danny could get down there by half seven. Then he'd help Kofi all he could. Because he was appalled by his story. He couldn't believe anyone could get away with what this agent had done to him.

And he was going to use all his skills as a detective to nail him.

'Who are you?'

Danny looked up. It was the boys from the playground. Five of them. They were holding cans and bottles. One who was a bit taller than the others was talking to him.

Great, Danny thought. But he stayed calm. That was the answer. Be calm. But be ready. To run.

Danny smiled up at the lads, then stood. He was about the same height as they were.

'I said, *Who are you?*'

'Danny,' he said. 'Danny Harte.'

Danny couldn't see their faces. Their hoods were up and the lights from the main road behind them were bright, making silhouettes of them.

And there was something else now. The police car that had seen Danny earlier had drawn up next to the playground. Two officers emerging, walking towards them. The other boys had not seen the car; they had their backs to it.

Danny made sure his hood was down and out

of sight. Then he took the book he'd been reading out of his bag and placed it on the bench next to him. He needed to make himself look different. Lose the hoody. A quick identity change and the police might not recognize him from earlier, down the hill.

'What's that?' the taller one sneered, looking at Danny's book.

Danny wondered how to respond. Normally in a situation like this he would try to escape, not make anyone angry. But with the police only a few seconds away he knew he was relatively safe. Then an idea came to him. A way to get himself out of both these situations. The gang and the police.

He would make himself look like a victim.

If he did, the police might see him in a different light. They'd never think of the boy they chased being the same one who was being bullied ten minutes and a kilometre later.

'Have you never seen one before?' Danny asked, answering the question at last. 'They're called books.'

Danny heard one of the gang laugh. The leader swung round and hit him on the mouth. None of the rest of the gang moved. Then the leader turned back to Danny.

'You're dead.'

Danny wondered what to do next. If he could just get the lad to push him over. Something minor. Not a punch. Just something so the police would come to his rescue. He could see that they were less than a hundred metres away now.

So Danny pushed the leader. Just a small shove. And he did it in a way the police wouldn't see him. Like a footballer getting a nudge into another player on the blind side of the referee.

The lad looked surprised. Like no one had ever pushed him before. And – like a child – he pushed Danny back. Not with massive force, but Danny saw the police were on them now, so he fell, gazing up at the gang.

'HEY! Stop that.'

The policeman had shouted. The gang turned round to see two policemen bearing down on them. They looked even more surprised now.

'What's going on?' the policeman said to Danny.

'Nothing,' Danny said.

'Nothing. Come on, son. What are they doing to you?'

'Nothing. We were just having a disagreement about this book.'

Danny heard another gang member laugh.

One of the policemen put his hand out. Danny took it and eased himself up.

He was safe. Now he had to get home on time and plan what he was going to say to Anton the next day.

WEDNESDAY

ACTION

Danny had set his alarm for 6 a.m. When it went off he got out of bed immediately. No lie-in.

He had to see Holt.

He put on his school uniform – stuffing his tie into his pocket – splashed his face with water and headed downstairs for the kitchen. He'd have a quick breakfast and leave the house before anyone else got up. Then he would try to think about what had happened the night before.

'Morning, Danny.'

Danny jumped and took a deep breath. Dad was sitting in the kitchen, his body silhouetted against the window.

'Hi, Dad,' Danny said, trying to sound normal.

'Where are you off to?'

Danny wondered if he should say he was up early to do some homework before setting off to school. But his dad always wanted the truth.

'I'm off to see Anton. Before school.'

'Social visit?'

'I want to talk to him about the takeover.' Danny poured his cereal and waited for the telling-off.

Dad nodded. 'It's looking more likely,' he said, without sounding like he was angry.

'I know,' Danny said. 'But if the fans . . .'

'If the fans can buy the club we can be the next Barcelona?' Dad finished his sentence.

'Exactly,' Danny said, smiling.

Dad stood up. 'You'll have to tell me what he says.'

'Mmm hmm.' Danny nodded, crunching his breakfast. He felt happy talking to his dad. This was the first conversation they'd had since he'd been arrested. He needed to talk to his dad like this. It made him feel good. It probably helped that Mum was away for work. Again.

'Dad?'

'Yeah.'

'I'm sorry about all this stuff recently. The police and that.'

'I know,' Dad said.

'I didn't mean it to go that far.'

'Neither did I, Danny.'

Danny was still thinking about what his dad had said when he walked down Wellington Street to the newspaper offices. What had he meant when he said, 'Neither did I'? Had he meant he was still disappointed in Danny? Or had he meant he wished he'd not had to ask Danny to take down his detective gear?

Danny wasn't sure.

It was 7.30 a.m. when he arrived. It was still murky-dark. But Danny knew Holt would be in his office already.

Danny called him. Holt picked up after the first ring and agreed to come down to see Danny, bringing two steaming cups of tea with him. Both in City FC mugs.

They sat on a wall, trains trundling on several tracks out of the station. Danny hoped Kofi would still be asleep, not as cold as he had looked last night when he'd left him at the industrial estate.

'Do you want the latest on the takeover?' Holt asked.

Danny nodded, looking up from his mug of tea.

'There was some meeting going on last night,' Holt said. 'A group of guys from somewhere. But the club wouldn't comment on it.'

'I see,' said Danny. He knew he'd been right about them.

'And I followed them last night.'

'Yeah?' Danny said, perking up. 'You should have called me!'

Holt raised an eyebrow.

Danny smiled. 'So what did you find out?'

'Not much. They left the airport late. I tried to find out where they were going back to, but they were on a private plane, not one of the scheduled flights.'

Danny frowned. That meant foreign investors. Probably.

'What about the fans' takeover?'

Holt laughed. 'You still think that's going to happen? It's a dream, Danny. There's no one with enough money to head it up. I'm sorry, Danny, you've had a wasted journey.'

They sat in silence, watching the trains go by. Danny was trying to get the right words to tell Holt about Kofi. Holt kept looking at him, like he was going to ask him a question. But neither spoke.

A long train arrived at the station. Danny gazed over at the City Stadium in the distance. He could just make out the warehouses and other buildings on the industrial estate.

'There's something else,' Danny said slowly.

'I knew there was,' Holt said. 'I knew it. I was just waiting.'

Danny grinned.

'Go on, then,' Holt said.

Danny was pleased Holt was so interested in him. He could have just treated him like most men in their twenties would treat a teenage boy. Like he was a kid. But Holt was OK. And that was partly because in the last few months Danny had brought Holt his two biggest scoops.

Danny glanced at the clock tower of the newspaper offices. A flickering electronic screen. He knew he didn't have much time. He wanted to take Kofi some breakfast before he headed off to school.

'There's a boy sleeping rough near the City Stadium,' Danny said. 'Kofi. He says he's from Ghana. He says an agent brought him over here to play for City. But that he cheated him –'

'Ghana?' Holt interrupted. 'Are you serious?'

'Yeah, he's . . .' And Danny repeated what Kofi had told him the night before.

'And he's sleeping rough? Just abandoned? How old is he?'

'Sixteen,' Danny answered, surprised how interested Holt had suddenly become.

'It's not happened here yet.'

'What?' Danny wasn't sure what Holt meant.

'This,' Holt went on. 'Taking young footballers from Africa to Europe, cheating them out of money. Trafficking!'

'There's a name for it?'

'There is, Danny. It's slavery. Well, modern slavery. Sort of.'

Danny shook his head.

'In France and Italy it's a massive problem,' Holt went on animatedly, 'and Belgium. I've read loads about it on the Internet. And the BBC did a documentary about it last year.'

Danny tried to bring Holt down. He seemed excited. And Danny was more worried about Kofi. What was going to happen to him next?

'So can you help him?'

'What?'

'Kofi?' Danny said. 'Can you help him?'

THURSDAY

KOFI'S STORY

The following morning Danny was outside the newsagent's before it opened. He wanted to be the first to read Anton's article.

It was still pitch black and cold as Danny watched the staff in the shop flicking the lights on, then gathering the bound-up bales of newspapers from the front door and cutting the plastic ties that held them together. Then the man who ran the newsagent's waved over to Danny. They knew each other. Danny bought *World Soccer* and *FourFourTwo* there every month. And before that he'd got *Match of the Day* and *Match*. When he was younger.

Outside, in the light of a street lamp, Danny read:

FOOTBALLER TRAFFICKED INTO UK – EXCLUSIVE

It's been a problem in Europe for years. Young African men trafficked in, cheated by men posing as football agents. In France alone there are over 7,000 young men living on the streets in poverty, young men who thought they were about to become among the richest men in Europe. Professional footballers.

But they were not. They had been cheated out of their money. Then left with nothing. And now, for the first time, the problem has hit the UK.

I met him on Wednesday. It was a clear morning, the sun shining. But it was cold and Kofi Danquah was shivering. He was sitting on a pile of pallets between two industrial units. In the shadow of the City Stadium. He eyed the stadium wistfully before he began to tell me his story.

'I am from Ghana,' he said. 'A football agent spotted me playing in Kumasi. He offered to take me to England, to play for City FC. In Ghana we all love City FC.'

That's because they all want to be the next Anthony Owusu.

'He asked my family for a fee. My family sold our farm. So we could pay him. Then I could come here and earn a lot of money. To send the money home. To change everybody's life.'

Kofi's family raised £6,000. In a country where the average wage is £300, his family gambled everything on getting Kofi here.

But they have lost.

'They think I am next coming home with a sports car and bags full of money,' Kofi said, casting his eyes down at the earth.

Kofi caught a flight to the UK two days ago. The agent said he would meet Kofi at the airport here and take him personally to City FC, his new team.

But there was no one to meet Kofi at the airport. Kofi called the agent. The agent said that City had been unable to find him a place. That he couldn't help him.

But speaking to City's youth coach, Sam Beckett, yesterday, I was assured they have no knowledge of Kofi Danquah.

So Kofi is stuck. He has no return ticket. He had expected to fly home in a private jet. Maybe a jet he could buy for himself. He has no visa to stay in the UK for a long time. No money. And worst of all he has no money to take home, no career to pay back his extended family in Ghana.

In France most of the 7,000 young men who have been trafficked in this way have been forced into illegal work. Many of them into crime, prostitution and worse.

Is this going to become a problem in the UK? Here in our city?

The name of Kofi's so-called agent is Jonathan

Shearer. We phoned Shearer asking for an interview, but he was unavailable to comment.

We wanted to ask him if Kofi is the first of these boys to be coming over to the UK. And whether there are more on the way. Is this, one of Europe's most shameful crimes, going to be something we hear a lot more of? And, if it is, what are we going to do about it?

Danny smiled. This was good. He knew Holt had put Kofi up in a local hotel. And, after that, surely someone would offer to help Kofi now. Maybe even City. They could fly him home.

Danny scanned the pages. He saw another piece by Anton.

TAKEOVER OVERTAKES FANS

Supporters who had been hoping to build enough momentum for a fans' takeover of City FC may be too late.

Events may have overtaken them.

Last night a group of international businessmen met at the City Stadium. They appeared to tour the stadium before gathering in a meeting room that overlooks the pitch. They then headed to the airport, where they left in a private jet.

The destination of that jet – which would possibly answer the question about who the next owners of City FC will be – remains a mystery.

Who were the group of men in suits seen at City yesterday?

Why is their identity being kept a secret by City FC's current owners?

What is about to happen to one of the UK's leading football clubs?

There are no answers. But the *Evening Post* hopes to have names in the next twenty-four hours.

Check out our website, www.eveningpost.co.uk/cityfc, and tomorrow's early editions for the latest news.

Danny frowned. Trying to help Kofi was satisfying. He'd been feeling better about himself. But this? This was bad news.

He walked home. He'd have his breakfast, then head off to Kofi's hotel before school. He wanted to show Kofi the newspaper article, see how he was feeling. And give him his phone back, now it was charged.

Then Danny's phone rang. He went to answer it, but realized it wasn't his. It was Kofi's that was ringing.

Danny flicked it open and looked at the number.

What should he do? Let it ring? Maybe Kofi would miss a vital call from his mum or someone. Danny had to decide. So he pressed Answer.

'Hello?'

'Danquah, you are a dead boy. I'm coming to get you.'

The voice was loud and furious – and carried a strange accent. Vicious. Danny didn't speak. He was paralysed with fear.

'You hear me, boy? Tell the newspaper man that if there are any more articles, I'll kill you all the more slowly. I'm in the city. Don't bother running. I'll find you.'

The line went dead.

Danny swallowed.

What was he going to tell Kofi now?

TERROR

Kofi opened his hotel room door cautiously when Danny knocked. He was staying in a budget hotel on the other side of the inner ring road, two hundred metres from the *Evening Post*'s offices.

'Danny!' Kofi said loudly when he saw who it was. He shook Danny's hand, then let him in.

Danny stepped inside, checking up and down the corridor before he did.

'Are you OK, Kofi?' Danny asked.

'Yes. Better. Thank you. You have helped me. And this hotel. It is beautiful.'

'Have you seen Anton's article?'

Kofi shrugged.

'The thing Anton wrote about you?' Danny went on.

'No,' Kofi replied, 'not yet.'

Danny handed the newspaper to Kofi. He realized he had twisted it into a tight roll.

Kofi read it quickly. Then he put the newspaper down and closed his eyes.

Danny said nothing for a moment. He could see that Kofi was breathing in and out. Quickly.

'What is it?' Danny asked.

After a pause, Kofi opened his eyes.

'This. At the end. About Mr Shearer . . .'

'Yes?' Danny asked, wondering when he should break the news to Kofi about the call he'd just had.

'It is not good.'

Danny nodded. He knew that. Now.

Kofi's mind was in a frenzy. He was remembering what he had heard about football agents at home. If you did as they asked everything was fine. They would get you a football club in Europe. They would make you rich. But if you didn't do what they asked . . . there were stories.

Kofi had heard about one family who confronted a so-called agent at one of Accra's academies. They said that he had cheated them out of money. Kofi had never believed it. Why would an agent find a player a club in Europe, then be accused of cheating them out of money?

It had ended badly. The family had been attacked. Their home burned down. Nobody could link it to the agent. But there were rumours.

Kofi had a gut feeling about this article: naming Jonathan Shearer was not a good thing. He was scared that something bad would happen. To him. Or, worse, to his family at home in Ghana.

Then he heard Danny speak.

'There's something else,' Danny said.

Kofi looked at Danny, again saying nothing.

'I had a call,' Danny said, 'on your mobile.'

Danny handed the phone back to Kofi.

'My family?' Kofi asked.

Danny shook his head. 'It was a man. With a deep voice.'

Danny watched Kofi check his mobile phone. To see the number that the call had come from.

It was Shearer's. He recognized it.

'What did he say?' Kofi asked.

Danny wasn't sure how he should reply. Should he tell Kofi everything? Or tone it down? To make him feel better.

Danny knew he had to do the right thing. He breathed in.

'The man said not to talk to the newspapers any more.' Danny paused again. He wanted to be completely upfront with Kofi. 'That he was coming to get you . . . to kill you.'

Two hundred metres away, underneath the *Evening Post* building, Anton Holt swung his bag into the back of his car. He was heading off to interview a player at City FC's training ground.

He was smiling. He was a happy man.

Today he'd had two stories in the paper. Two

big stories. A scoop about something that had never been reported in the UK before and an investigative piece about an ongoing story. One he was sure was going to develop. And one he was sure that he was going to be at the centre of: the inevitable takeover of City FC.

He glanced up when he heard a Transit van edging through the car park. He was surprised to see one down here. There were no pick-ups due from the newspaper at this time: all the early editions would be in the newsagents' by now. Then he smiled again. It must be an extra van. They must be printing more papers. Because of his story.

Holt stepped close to his car, half shutting the door, to allow the van to pass him.

As he did the van stopped. A man got out.

'Can you help me?' the man said, not in a local voice.

'Sure,' Anton said, smiling. 'Are you looking for the loading bay?'

Thinking back, Holt would remember the moment he said this. That at the same time he heard the back doors of the van open and feet landing on the tarmac. But he hadn't registered it. He was too busy talking to the man in front of him.

The next thing that happened was that he was

grabbed from behind, then plunged into semi-darkness. And he could hardly breathe.

It took a few seconds to realize there was a sack over his head. And that he had been punched or kicked hard in his side. So hard that he had to spend all his energy trying to catch his breath, trying to breathe in, then out.

As he did this he heard the van rev its engine and felt his body roll to hit the side of what he assumed was the van.

Then he blacked out.

'You have to tell Anton,' Danny said to Kofi.

But Kofi was not listening. He was stuffing his few clothes into his bag.

'Kofi!'

'No,' Kofi said, quiet and calm. But Danny could tell he was terrified.

'What are you doing?'

'Leaving here.'

'To where?'

'Leaving here,' Kofi repeated.

'Anton can help.'

'No,' Kofi said again, moving past Danny to the door, then stopping. He turned to face Danny. 'You have tried to help me. Thank you.'

Danny said nothing. He wondered if he *had*

helped. Or if he'd made things a lot worse for Kofi.

Neither boy said anything until Kofi put out his hand for Danny to shake.

Danny shook it.

Then Kofi left, his bag hanging from his right hand, leaving Danny alone in the hotel room wondering what the hell he should do next.

TRAPPED

Danny walked as fast as he could without running. Even though he had some terrifying thoughts going round his head, he needed to get to school. This would be worse if he didn't make it look to his family and teachers like everything was normal.

He had never walked to school from the city centre before. It was a different route from the one he'd take home. He could have caught a bus, but he wanted to walk, to think, to get his head straight.

He'd rarely been in the city centre so early on a weekday. Only when he was doing a work placement at the newspaper with Anton a couple of months ago. There were hundreds of people streaming from the railway station, most of them dressed in black. People of all ages, from not much older than Danny to as old as his grandad, walked en masse from the station, then in smaller and smaller groups up side streets and over roads, disappearing into buildings.

To work, Danny thought.

And he shuddered. He hated the idea that after school he would join this mass of people getting off trains and buses, walking into buildings, to offices, computer screens and fifteen-minute tea breaks. He wanted more than that. He wanted every day to be different. A new crime to solve every week.

But he knew he had to think, not about this but about his problem. Kofi's problem. Danny wanted to know, most of all, where Kofi had gone.

After leaving the hotel, Kofi could have gone anywhere in the city. He could be alone – with the threat hanging over him that someone wanted to find him. To kill him.

And to make it worse, if it could be any worse, some of this was Danny's fault. If he hadn't led Holt to Kofi only half of these things would be happening. He had thought, at the time, it was the right thing to do. Now he wasn't so sure.

Danny was confused. And what he liked to do when he was confused was talk to someone.

Normally his dad.

But his mum had banned him from detective work. So that was out.

Then there was Charlotte. But she wasn't talking to him.

So Danny decided to call Anton. He was the obvious choice anyway. Danny speed-dialled the journalist. The phone rang six times, then went dead. Danny rang again. This time there was only the message: *The person you are telephoning is not available. Please try again later.*

What was Holt up to? Surely he'd be at the paper by now? Like he had been yesterday.

About a kilometre away, across the city, a white van arrived at the far end of the IKEA car park. At the very edge of the car park there were two huge metal boxes. Containers. The kind you see on the backs of lorries. Or stacked ten high on massive container ships.

The van stopped, then reversed up to one of the containers. A man climbed out of the van and opened a large padlock on the front of the container. Then he banged on the back of the van.

Nobody watched as three men bundled a fourth into the container. Nobody saw the door padlocked again before the van moved off.

And nobody knew that the *Evening Post*'s chief sports writer was inside the container. In the dark. Without food or water. Without a phone. Without hope.

As he approached school Danny changed his route, wanting to walk the way he knew Charlotte came into school.

There were streams of children heading into

school. *A bit like the adults streaming out of the station in town*, Danny thought. And for the first time that day he felt tired. Tired because he'd been up too late, then up too early. Tired because he'd been thinking about Kofi and everything else.

Danny phoned Charlotte.

It rang three times, then went dead.

Danny sighed. She had hung up on him again. He put the phone to his forehead. He didn't like this. He needed to be friends with Charlotte. Without having her there, something inside him felt wrong.

Then he heard her voice.

He put the phone to his ear. 'Charlotte?'

He heard laughing. He looked at his phone. And for a moment he was completely disoriented.

Then the laughing was louder.

Not coming from the phone. He knew that now.

He closed his eyes and slipped his phone into his pocket. Then he turned. And there was Charlotte. With Sally Graham and Rebecca Page. Standing outside a newsagent's.

And he knew what he was going to do next was important. He missed having Charlotte as a friend. He needed her. So he had to play this right.

FRIENDS

'Hello,' Charlotte said, her laugh faltering.

'Hi,' Danny replied.

He looked at Charlotte. He could tell she was still cross with him. There was something in her eyes. He knew her by now. He watched her putting a small file into her school bag.

'What are they?' he asked.

'Leaflets,' she said blankly.

'What for?'

Sally Graham cut in. 'She's been badgering shopkeepers again. Sell fair-trade chocolate or she'll make everyone in school stop going there.'

'Not quite,' Charlotte said. 'I just gave them a leaflet to tell them about it. And tell them I'll not be shopping there until they sell it.'

'Good,' Danny said.

He walked alongside her, not sure what to say next. He wanted her on his own. Then he could talk through what was going on with Kofi. He needed her advice. Without her or his dad to talk to, he felt lost.

But something strange happened next.

Sally Graham was suddenly alongside him and she had linked her arm round his. It had happened in a second. With no warning.

Danny didn't know what to do. He wanted to pull his arm away. But he wasn't sure if he should. Sally was probably taking the mickey out of him, *expecting* him to pull his arm away. So he just walked along, trying to catch Charlotte's eye.

'So, Danny Harte,' Sally said, 'what are you doing tomorrow? It's a day off school. Inset day, remember? Maybe we could hook up?'

Danny still didn't know how to react. This was a wind-up, he was sure. Sally was pretending to fancy him, so they could all have a laugh at his expense when he took it seriously or pulled away.

Then he saw – to his other side – that Charlotte looked mad. Really mad. But that she was keeping it inside, not letting it out. And Danny realized that, if this was a joke, Charlotte was not in on it.

So he made a decision.

He pulled his arm away. Gently, but firmly.

'I'm going to the cinema with Charlotte,' he said.

At first there was a little silence. Then Danny felt Charlotte's shoulder leaning into his. Danny realized that Sally *had* been serious. And that he appeared, for once, to have done the right thing.

*

'I'm still cross with you.'

'I know,' Danny said. 'I'm sorry.'

'But thanks for doing what you did with Sally.'

Danny wanted to say it was OK, but he wasn't sure if he should. So he just nodded.

Neither of them spoke. They were sitting in the stairwell, alone. Deeply uncomfortable with the silence, Danny had no idea what to do next.

'I need your help,' he blurted out, above the noise of a class thundering down the staircase above them.

'With what?'

'With this thing . . .'

'Thing?'

'There's this lad . . .'

'Is this another of your investigations, Danny?'

'It is,' Danny said, 'but not the takeover.'

'Then what?'

So Danny told her. About finding Kofi. Everything that had happened from finding him and setting him up with Holt to Kofi disappearing with a death threat hanging over him.

'You have to call Anton,' Charlotte said as soon as he stopped talking.

Danny nodded. 'I've tried,' he said. 'But his line's dead.'

'Won't he be at the paper?'

'He should be.'

'What about the police?'

'What about them?'

'Why don't you go to them?' Charlotte asked.

'Because I think I need to talk to Anton first.'

Charlotte stopped talking for a second, then started again.

'OK,' she said, 'then you have to go to him.' She sounded so bothered that Danny felt quite pleased.

'Will you come?' Danny said.

'Me?'

'Yeah.'

'Why?'

'Because . . .' Danny said. 'Because I want you to.'

'OK.'

'After school?'

'OK.'

Danny grinned.

'But, Danny,' Charlotte said, suddenly looking worried.

'Yeah?'

'What about the cinema? Tomorrow?'

Danny looked at Charlotte. What was going on? Her face looked serious. So he tried to look serious too. Then – after an agonizing pause – Charlotte pushed him against the wall, started laughing and ran upstairs.

Danny sighed in relief and followed Charlotte upstairs to their first class.

COVER-UP

Charlotte and Danny got the bus into town after school. They were outside the *Evening Post* offices well before 4 p.m.

'Shall we just check if Kofi's gone back to his hotel room?' Danny asked.

'Good thinking.'

They walked in the direction of the hotel. Under the inner ring road. The air was poisonous with exhaust fumes because of a traffic jam. Danny could hear horns beeping as drivers became more and more impatient.

They walked into the hotel. To the reception desk in the cramped entrance. Not a posh hotel, like the ones he'd seen in Moscow.

'Excuse me. Is your guest Kofi Danquah still here, please?' Danny asked the receptionist, wondering if he sounded too formal, as he was never sure how to behave in hotels.

The receptionist checked a list. 'No,' she said. 'He left unexpectedly this morning. But he's still got unlimited nights left here. We've kept his room for him.'

'Right, thanks,' Danny said.

'Are you with the other guy?' the receptionist said.

'Anton Holt?' Danny asked, assuming Holt had been in to call for Kofi.

'Yeah, the older guy.'

Danny nodded. 'Sort of,' he said, and made for the door.

But something stopped him.

Older guy?

He was about to laugh and remember to tell Holt he'd been called 'older'. It was a strange phrase for a man in his twenties.

Danny backtracked. There was a tiny question in his mind. And he knew, from having read a hundred crime novels, that even the tiniest question had to be followed up.

He headed back to the desk, leaving Charlotte holding the door, puzzled.

'This older guy?' Danny asked the receptionist.

'Yeah?'

'How much *older* was he?'

'White hair,' the receptionist said quickly. 'Posh suit. Funny accent.'

Danny nodded. 'And he was the only one in asking for Kofi?'

'Yeah,' the receptionist said, smiling uneasily. 'You're starting to sound like a policeman.'

'Thanks,' Danny said. For him that was a compliment.

'Listen,' the receptionist said, 'seeing as you're his friend, you'd better take this.' She handed Danny Kofi's mobile phone.

Danny looked at it, puzzled.

'He left it,' she said. 'On the bed. I'm surprised he didn't see it when he left.'

'The guy the receptionist mentioned,' Danny said to Charlotte, as they walked back under the inner ring road.

'What about him?'

'He must be the agent.'

'I suppose he must,' Charlotte agreed.

'That's not good,' said Danny.

He looked around to see if there was someone with white hair and a posh suit hanging around.

There wasn't.

'We need to talk to Holt.'

'I know.'

They walked towards the *Evening Post* building. The sky had darkened since they left school and now the first drops of rain had begun to fall. Most of the front of the building was glass and Danny noticed flecks of rain making a sweeping pattern on it.

Then he noticed the police van. And six policemen standing across the front of the building.

Instinctively, Danny took Charlotte's arm. Just like this morning.

She looked at him, half smiling, half puzzled.

'There are police everywhere,' Danny said.

'Aren't there always?' Charlotte said.

'No.'

'I see.'

Danny and Charlotte carried on walking. Up to the revolving doors.

'ID please,' a police officer said, stopping them and moving her body between them and the door.

'I don't have any,' Danny said.

'It's limited access, sir,' the policewoman said.

'I'm here to see a reporter.'

'Have you got an appointment?'

'No.'

'It's limited access, then, sir.'

'So we can't come in?'

'I'm afraid not, sir.'

Danny wasn't sure which was the most unsettling thing: his worries about Kofi or this policewoman calling him 'sir' all the time.

'What's going on, then?' Danny asked.

'There's no information at the moment, sir.'

Danny nearly smiled. He could have been talking to a robot, not a human being.

He sighed. 'Thanks anyway.'

Danny and Charlotte walked away from the newspaper building.

'What's all that about?' Charlotte asked.

'I don't know.'

'What are you going to do?'

'Wait,' Danny said.

'Why?'

'If you just wait and watch,' Danny replied, 'something sometimes happens.'

They waited on the edge of a small car park at the front of the building. It was not the main car park where, Danny knew, Holt parked his car. It was the car park for the newspaper's editor, Giles Forshaw, and visiting VIPs. It seemed to Danny a good place to watch who entered and left the building. He needed to work out why there was a police presence at the *Evening Post* on the day that Kofi Danquah had disappeared.

Thirty minutes later Danny got what he wanted. Someone was walking towards them. Someone he recognized. One of Holt's sports-writing team. Ellen Droad.

'Danny,' she said, approaching quickly. 'I saw you from upstairs.'

'Hello,' Danny said.

He knew Ellen from the offices where Holt worked. From when he had been on a work placement there.

Ellen was breathless. She smiled quickly at Charlotte, then glanced round at the police who were manning the doors.

'Anton's been taken.'

'What?' Danny said.

'He was taken from the car park. We've got it on CCTV. In a white van. Do you know *anything*? About the takeover? They think he's been taken because he was about to spill the beans. That he'd found something out.'

Danny shook his head. In disbelief.

'No. All I know is what I read in the paper. That he knew something. That he was about to announce it.'

Ellen looked at the floor, then up at the building. Danny could see her eyes welling with tears.

'He'll be OK,' Danny reassured her, before he even knew what he was saying.

Ellen shrugged.

And Danny wished he'd not spoken. Because he

wasn't sure – not sure at all – that Anton *would* be OK. In fact, he had a feeling of dread that made him worry that it would definitely *not* be OK.

FRIDAY

IN THE DARK

Holt sat without moving. When he had come round he had absolutely no idea where he was.

It was pitch black. The floor and the wall were cold metal beneath and behind him.

He could hear cars racing past, but they were very muffled.

His senses were hyper-alert, picking up everything. Anything. Something that he could use to help make sense of what had happened.

What he knew was that he was in some sort of room. Probably a prefabricated hut, like a Portakabin. He knew that he had an extreme pain in his head. And he knew that he had been attacked, abducted and now – no doubt – was a prisoner.

But there was also a lot he didn't know.

Where he was. Why he was here. How long he'd been here. And how he was going to get out.

It did occur to him that he might not get out. Ever. But that thought filled him with such fear and panic that he had to suppress it, think of something else.

He tried to think clearly.

Why would he be abducted and imprisoned?

Something to do with his new girlfriend? No. She was an ordinary nice girl. No mafia connections there.

Something to do with the five-a-side match he'd been involved in last week, when it'd got a bit nasty? No, it was only football.

What did that leave?

His job?

That was it. He had been taken because of his job.

So why would a journalist be abducted?

Well, it happened a lot in other countries. They were tortured in Myanmar. Murdered in the street in Russia. Arrested and imprisoned in China.

And why?

Because they wrote about things people didn't want them to write about.

Then Anton realized why he was here. It was obvious.

Because he had written about the City takeover. Because he was on to something.

But what?

Who would go to the extreme of kidnapping him?

And what would they do with him?

Again the thought that he might be here forever,

locked in a metal box and left to die, began to take over his mind. He was terrified. That he could be here day after day, slowly dying.

Anton stopped himself. His ears had picked up something new. The noise of the cars was the same in the background. But in the foreground he could hear one car, a louder engine, the sound of heavy tyres on tarmac.

Then the noise stopped.

Was someone coming?

Holt felt his way up the metal wall and stood. He wanted to be standing if someone came in. He didn't know why. He just had to be on his feet.

He heard loud metal clanging noises next. The door. Someone was opening the door to this prison. He covered his eyes as the headlights of a van shone into the container, blinding him. He couldn't see. Apart from two silhouettes breaking the light.

'You are Anton Holt,' one of the two men said. 'You are the chief sports writer on the *Evening Post*. You support City FC. You were born in the city, have always lived in the city, apart from three years studying to become a journalist in Darlington. Your mother and father moved to Cumbria two years ago, after your mother retired. She was a teacher. Your father was a welder. They live at The Cottage,

Lakeview Crescent, Lindale, Cumbria. Yesterday they spent most of their time in the garden, tending to their plants.'

Now that he could see properly, Anton looked at both men. One had silver hair and what could have been a South African accent. He was tall and thin. His skin leathery. The other man was tall too, but muscular, tattooed and dressed head to foot in black.

Anton shivered. He thought of his parents and the fact that this man was clearly a threat to them. They were old. He felt a fierce aggression building in his arms and legs. But he knew better than to show it. The bigger man would crush him in a second.

'What have you done to them?' Anton said, his voice cracking as it was the first thing he'd said since he had been taken.

'Nothing,' the silver-haired man said. 'Yet.'

Anton nodded. 'What do you want?' he asked.

He knew there would be a demand – stop following the story about the City takeover. Or else.

But the silver-haired man surprised him.

'What else have you written about Kofi Danquah?'

'What?' Holt asked, genuinely surprised.

'Danquah?' the man repeated. 'Have you written any more? Is there more to come out?'

Although Holt was keen to say things that would please the man who had his life in his hands, he knew he needed to be careful. If he said he had written nothing, the man might kill him. Or just leave him here. If he said he had written more but that its publication could be stopped, it might help save him.

And why was he asking about this? Was this man something to do with Kofi's story? Was he the agent behind it all? Was *this* the reason for his kidnap? Nothing to do with the club takeover at all?

Anton knew he had to reply quickly. And to appear scared to death. Which would not be difficult: because he was.

'I have a couple of articles ready to go,' Anton said. 'I did some research. There's more.'

The silver-haired man nodded. 'Maybe,' he said. 'But maybe not.'

Anton said nothing. He felt utterly helpless.

'I will wait to see what happens before I kill you,' the man said. 'I may need you later. So no death yet.'

The man smiled. He was enjoying his power.

Anton tried to breathe in and out slowly. To keep calm.

He eyed the door. Could he get out?

'I am Jonathan Shearer,' the man said. 'I bring boys from Ghana to Europe. I tell them they have a place at a big club. Like AC Milan, Barcelona. I take money off them. Then I take their money. Like Kofi Danquah.' He went on. 'And don't look at the door. Don't think of escaping. Bjorn here will kill you without a second thought. How will your parents feel? Their son missing, no body, just the faint smell of a corpse at the side of a motorway for a couple of weeks.'

Anton nodded again. He did not want to hear what this man was telling him. He knew that, by giving him all this detail, Jonathan Shearer would not let him go now. He really was intending to kill him. That was why he could be so open. He was actually boasting!

'Your story. About Kofi. It will cost me money. I was hoping to take my business into the UK. The governments in Italy and Belgium and France are making things difficult for me.' Shearer paused. 'Or do you think your newspaper will be happy to retract the story you wrote about poor Kofi Danquah?'

Hearing Shearer's question, Anton looked up.

SHEARER AGAIN

Danny and Charlotte were in the city centre now.
In a café. At first Danny had suggested they go to
Starbucks, where they had been before together
and where he sometimes went with his dad. But
Charlotte had shook her head.

'I don't want to. Let's go to that fair-trade café
down the bottom of town,' she'd said.

'The Bear?'

'Yeah.'

Danny smiled as he sipped his Coke. 'You're well
into this fair-trade thing, aren't you?'

'Aren't *you*?' Charlotte asked, looking straight
at him.

'I think I need to know more,' he replied, still
smiling.

Then Kofi's phone vibrated in his pocket.

Danny answered without pausing. He knew who
it was. He was scared, but he also knew he needed
to take the call. For Anton's sake.

'Hello.'

'Kofi?' A sharp accented voice struck Danny's
ear.

'No,' Danny said guardedly.

'Ah, so it's Danny?'

Danny nearly dropped the phone. How on earth did this so-called football agent know *his* name?

He decided to say nothing.

Shearer spoke again. 'Danny Harte. Schoolboy. City FC fan. Friend of Kofi Danquah.'

Danny stayed quiet. But he wanted to get something out of this call. Something about Anton.

'Yes?' Danny said.

Then he realized he was staring into Charlotte's eyes.

'What?' she mouthed.

Danny mouthed back, *Shearer!*

'Pass me to Kofi,' Shearer ordered, the sound of a seagull coming over the phone as well as the dangerous voice.

'He's not here,' Danny said back.

'Get him.'

'I don't know where he is,' Danny said. 'Where is Anton Holt?'

What else was that he could hear? A road. The sound of cars whooshing past. Lots of them.

'So you know Holt too?' Shearer said. 'Of course.'

'Where is he?' Danny's voice was cracking with fear. And he knew that Shearer would be sensing that fear.

'Listen to me. You and Kofi *and* Holt will all be dead if this mess is not sorted out.'

Danny tried to speak. But he couldn't. His throat was too dry. But he could hear. A third sound. A beep-beep-beeping. A lorry or a bus reversing.

'Tomorrow the *Evening Post* will retract its story about me,' Shearer went on. 'And you and Kofi will not contradict that retraction. Don't even think about going to the police. If you do, Anton Holt will die. And so will you.'

Danny was out of his depth. He wished he could talk to Anton to ask him what was the best thing to do.

He felt lost, hopeless.

Then he looked down at the table. Something was touching him.

Charlotte had her hand on his.

And somehow it gave him strength. A way to speak.

'OK,' he said. That was the right thing to say. Placate the kidnapper. Try to do something to help Anton.

Then the line was dead.

After pausing, the mobile to his ear, Danny placed it softly on the table in front of him.

'What was that?' Charlotte said slowly.

'Shearer,' he said.

Charlotte looked worried, then looked down at her hand on his. Danny noticed that she looked genuinely surprised that it was there. She withdrew it.

'What did he say?' she asked.

'He's got Anton.'

Charlotte nodded.

Danny didn't know what to say next. This was a dangerous situation. Like the ones he'd been in before. Each time he'd got into things this deep he'd *thought* his way out of it. But now it wasn't just him. Anton was involved too.

And Kofi.

And Charlotte.

MAP-READING

They met at Paul's house. His mum and dad were at work.

'So why can't we go to the police?' Paul asked.

'He says he'll kill us and Kofi and Anton if we do,' Danny said.

'But is that true?' Paul pressed. 'I mean, isn't that only what happens in films and books? Shouldn't we just go to the police?'

Paul was looking at Charlotte. Hoping she'd agree with him.

They were in the kitchen, with wooden units that surrounded an oval table. The window blind was down.

'It's up to Danny,' Charlotte said. 'He's done this before.'

Charlotte and Paul looked at Danny. And he wondered if he'd been right to ask his friends for their help. He normally had Anton with him when he was trying to solve these crimes. But now the crime *was* Anton. His abduction. And Danny needed help, most definitely. He could not do this on his own.

'If we go to the police,' Danny said, 'Shearer might know. He seems to know a lot.' He turned to Paul. 'He could have someone feeding him information from inside the police.'

'Or the newspaper?' Charlotte added.

Danny nodded.

Paul was silent for a moment. Then he said, 'I'll be honest. I'm scared.'

'Me too,' Danny agreed. 'But what else can we do?'

The three of them sat quietly for several seconds. Until Paul spoke.

'OK,' he said. 'I'll help.'

Danny wasn't sure what it was that had changed Paul's mind, but he was glad.

'Me too,' Charlotte said.

'Thank you.'

'So what now?' Paul asked. 'What do you need us to do?'

'Have you got a map of the city?'

'My mum has,' Paul said, and he disappeared.

Charlotte and Danny listened to his footsteps on the floor above. Danny glanced at Charlotte, feeling he should fill the silence with something clever or funny. Charlotte looked back at him. But nothing came to mind, so Danny looked at the kitchen table, feeling slightly ridiculous. He was relieved to then hear Paul's footsteps coming back down the stairs.

Paul burst back into the kitchen and tossed a folded map to Danny.

Danny opened it and laid it out on the kitchen table.

'So what's the map for?' Charlotte asked.

'We need to find Anton.'

'And?'

'And when Shearer phoned I heard noises in the background,' Danny said. 'He's obviously got him held somewhere. And I was thinking that maybe the noises would help. I read a novel once. A detective overheard the sound of boats and a foghorn over a phone. It helped him find a criminal. By the sea.'

'But the sea is over a hundred kilometres away,' Paul pointed out, smiling.

Danny smiled too. He knew his friend was trying to lighten the atmosphere.

'Shut up, Paul,' Charlotte said. 'What did you hear, Danny?'

'Three things. Heavy traffic moving fast. A lorry or bus reversing. And a seagull.

'So we look at the map and find places where you could hear all three things. Paul?' Danny turned to his friend. 'Can we draw on the map? I'll replace it.'

'Sure,' Paul said.

Danny took a black felt-tip pen out of his bag.

'Draw round all the motorways,' Charlotte said.

Danny nodded and drew channels across the map where motorways cut south, east and west of the city.

'There's the inner ring road too,' Paul said. 'That's fast. Like a motorway.'

Danny followed the instructions. The map was now cut up with black lines. Danny started to cross out anywhere not within a kilometre of a motorway.

'Now we're looking for seagulls and buses and lorries,' he said. 'So where would they be?'

'Buses could be anywhere,' Paul said.

'True,' Danny said. 'But reversing buses – or lorries – are normally in depots. We need to focus on them. We have to try to whittle it down.'

Charlotte nodded.

They all scanned the map. Picking out bus depots and industrial estates. Danny circled them all.

There were nineteen places.

'We can't watch nineteen places,' Paul said. 'We need three.'

'What about the seagulls?' Charlotte said. 'Where are they going to be?'

'Rubbish,' Danny answered.

'What?'

'Rubbish dumps.'

'And ploughed fields,' Charlotte added.

Then everyone was scanning the map again. Looking for dumps and fields near motorways and bus depots.

Eventually they came up with five places where you might be able to hear all three things. All near motorways. All near rubbish dumps. All near industrial estates or bus depots.

'Five places. Three of us,' Charlotte said.

Danny nodded. He knew they could only choose three. But what if they missed the right one?

He was aware that the other two were looking at him. They were ready to go with what he decided. The thought pleased him, but also embarrassed him. So he made a decision.

'We each choose the place that is right to us,' he said. 'Go with your instincts. Don't talk about it. Just choose.'

Danny liked making gut decisions as well as working things out. Sometimes a decision based on a hunch was right. Because it was your unconscious mind deciding. Not your conscious mind. Just like the detective Wallander, Danny thought.

Charlotte went immediately for the IKEA car park, slightly out of town.

Paul for the bus depot.

Danny chose the industrial estate near the football stadium.

And he tried to forget about the other two sites. For now.

'That's it, then,' Charlotte said.

Danny could hear that she sounded nervous. He knew he had to set her mind at rest. And Paul's. He wanted them to know that he wasn't putting them in danger. Just asking them to do some surveillance.

'All we are going to do is watch,' Danny said. 'That's it.'

'Watch?'

'We each take one place,' Danny said. 'You find somewhere where you can be hidden, then watch. Don't wear bright clothes. And take notes if you need to. Put your phones on silent. I'll call each of you every fifteen minutes. If I don't call for half an hour, call each other.'

'And what if we see something?' Charlotte asked.

'Call me. We'll all converge on the same spot.'

'Converge?' Paul asked. 'You sound like a war-film general.'

Danny said nothing for a moment. Then Charlotte was laughing. And Paul.

Danny smiled. He knew why they were laughing. Not because anything was funny. But because they were all terrified.

THREE DETECTIVES

The first thing Danny did when he reached the industrial estate was check the place he'd found Kofi. Just in case. But Kofi was not there.

Danny wondered where he was. In his mind he liked to picture Kofi arriving back in Ghana, at the airport, his family welcoming him home. But he knew that was a fairy tale.

It was more likely that Kofi was sleeping rough somewhere. Or that he had moved on. To escape Shearer. To London maybe.

But Kofi *was* on the industrial estate. He'd been there all night. When he'd arrived, after leaving the hotel, he had checked all the buildings. Just in case one of them was open. He was desperate to get out of the cold: he had never known such temperatures, never felt so uncomfortable.

He had noticed several of the units were 'To Let', as the signs said. He worked out that this meant there was no one using them.

Maybe if one of them had been left unsecured.

Kofi had tried doors and grilles, feeling guilty.

He didn't want to break in and steal anything. He wasn't a burglar. He just wanted to escape the cold. And maybe have a wash. But most of all he wanted to think.

Reaching one unit, he noticed a window that was not flush with the wall. Checking, he found that it *was* open. Kofi had tried over a hundred doors and windows and he couldn't quite believe this was happening.

He gently eased the window open, glanced around the industrial estate, then climbed in.

The space was empty. White walls. Grey floors. No furniture. No boxes of anything. Just scraps of rubbish in corners. And dead leaves. But there was a toilet. And running water. At least he was only hungry now. Not thirsty too.

Kofi knew that he had to think. To work things out.

What should he do?

Shearer was on the loose. And, according to Danny, after him.

So he should run. Get away. Surely. He must leave the city. Go to London.

But what about Danny? Didn't he owe Danny something?

Maybe. But, Kofi thought, Danny might be better off if he left for London. If Kofi left Danny would not be in harm's way. Shearer would leave the city. Everyone would be safe. Kofi was the one who had caused all this trouble. He could stop it too.

That was it. He'd leave. It'd be good for him, good for Danny, good for everyone.

He'd just get one night's sleep here. Then he'd go.

Danny climbed a slope to be above the industrial estate. Somewhere he could watch from. Then he listened. He could hear cars on the motorway. And, after a few minutes, a lorry reversing. Maybe he was in the right place. All he needed now was a seagull.

Danny phoned Charlotte.

'Where are you?' he asked.

'In IKEA,' she replied. 'Looking at cushions.'

'What!' Danny said, raising his voice.

Charlotte said nothing.

'You're not really in IKEA, are you?'

'No. I'm between two abandoned containers at the back of the car park.'

Danny could hear the noise of the motorway from where Charlotte was. Then a seagull.

'A seagull!' he said, excited. 'A seagull.'

'I know,' Charlotte said. 'Have you got seagulls?'

'No,' Danny answered. 'Charlotte?'

'Yes.'

'Be careful.'

Charlotte paused. Then she said, 'I will. You too.'

During the call, Danny had the strange feeling that he was being watched. Just a gut feeling. He moved slightly to make sure he wasn't standing out. The last thing he needed now was to be arrested. Again.

Next, after watching a lorry unloading pallets in his industrial estate, Danny called Paul. Again he could hear the noise of the road in the background.

'Anything?'

'No,' Paul said. 'Just buses coming and going.'

Danny heard the distinctive beep-beep-beep of a bus reversing.

'Hear that?' Paul asked.

'I did.'

'Danny?'

'What?'

'What should I be looking for?'

Danny wondered what to say for a moment. 'Just watch for what's normal. The bus drivers coming and going. There'll be patterns. Once you know what the patterns are, what the drivers and other staff do, you start to notice things that are different. That's what we're looking for. Anything different.'

'OK,' Paul said. 'But I don't think there's anything dodgy going on here.'

'You never know,' Danny said.

'Over and out,' Paul said in a funny voice.

Then Danny sat back on the hill, concealed partly by a bush. The afternoon wore on. He still couldn't shift the uneasy feeling that he was being watched, but he saw nothing suspicious.

Two hours in, still on the hill, his phone started vibrating.

At first he was filled with horror. That it was Shearer again. But he realized it was his phone, not Kofi's.

It was Charlotte.

'You OK?' Danny asked.

'There's something going on,' Charlotte was whispering.

'What?' Danny whispered back automatically.

'I'm not sure. Some men in a flash car. Circling the car park. Not shoppers. They're definitely up to something.'

'Where are you?'

'Where I said before. The IKEA car park. Two containers.'

'Stay there. We're coming.'

Danny cut Charlotte and called Paul. 'Charlotte's got something. Can you be at IKEA in twenty minutes?'

Paul said he could.

Then Danny was running. Down the road away from the City Stadium. And he wasn't sure if he was running because he wanted to solve this crime or because he wanted to make sure Charlotte was OK.

CHARLOTTE DISAPPEARS

As he got into his stride, coming down the hill, Danny caught something out of the corner of his eye. In a window. A movement. A flash of light.

He ran on for a few seconds. Then slowed.

Could it be?

Danny walked slowly back to the window. He peered in. But there was nothing there. And Danny wondered if he was seeing things he wanted to see: not real things.

'Kofi?' he said gently.

No reply. Just the noise of the motorway. The noise of the seagulls.

He turned to go. Back up the road to IKEA. And there, in front of him, was Kofi, trying, but failing, to smile.

Danny couldn't help grinning, even though he was worried about Charlotte. At least he'd found Kofi.

Danny explained to Kofi what was going on as they ran. About Holt. About Charlotte and Paul.

Danny didn't ask what Kofi had been up to. He

knew that if Kofi wanted to tell him about it, he would.

When Danny and Kofi arrived at IKEA, Paul was already there. They knew they had the right place: two containers, close together, in the IKEA car park. It matched Charlotte's description exactly.

Except that Charlotte wasn't there.

'Where is she?' Danny asked.

'I got here a minute ago,' Paul replied, looking at Kofi, smiling.

'This is Kofi,' Danny said to Paul. 'He was at the industrial estate.'

Paul and Kofi nodded to each other, then both were looking at Danny. He seemed distraught. Not bothered with making introductions. It was hardly the time.

The car park was packed. There were hundreds of cars. Dozens of people.

Danny pulled out his phone to call Charlotte again. But then he stopped. If she was in danger, he didn't want her answering to give away where she was.

'Let's search,' Danny said.

Neither of the others answered him. They were just waiting to be told what to do.

'But where?' Paul said eventually. 'There are so many people, so many cars and shops.'

'I don't know,' Danny said quietly.

His mind was going mad. Where was Charlotte? Was she in danger? And, if she was, how would he ever forgive himself? He was mad to get her involved in this.

In fact, he was mad to involve anyone else in these things. Maybe he was mad to get involved in them himself. He used to find this exciting. But now, because he'd put other people in danger, he was beginning to wonder if his dad had been right.

Where was she? And where was Jonathan Shearer? The thought that he might have something to do with Charlotte not being where she said she'd be was too much to bear.

'Danny,' Paul said, 'what shall we do?'

THE PLAN

The light caught Danny's eyes a couple of times before he thought it might mean something.

In a car park light can come off the windows and mirrors of moving cars all the time on a sunny day. It can blind you.

Danny stared in the direction of the flashing light. He was blinded, actually feeling pain from the effect of the light in his eyes.

'It's Charlotte,' Danny said. 'It must be.'

'Where?' Paul asked.

'I don't know. Where's the light coming from?'

Kofi pointed at a cluster of white vans. 'There is a woman,' he said, 'over there.'

The three boys walked towards the white vans. When Danny saw that Charlotte was standing behind one of them, hidden in the shade, he felt a rush of adrenalin. It *was* Charlotte. And she was OK.

They gathered behind one of the vans, as Charlotte drew them out of the sun, gesturing that they hide.

'There's something going on with the containers,' she said.

Danny interrupted. 'This is Kofi, by the way.'

'Hello, Kofi. I'm Charlotte. It's really good to see you safe.'

Kofi shook her hand.

'I heard something. A knocking in the containers. I was just standing there, being casual. Then two men came past in a silver Mercedes and gave me a funny look. I didn't think much of it. Until they came round again. And that was when I heard something knocking. From inside the container.'

'Brilliant,' Danny said, holding his hand up. 'This could be it. The sounds from the call from Shearer are all here.'

And it was true. They had heard the road, seagulls and lorries reversing since they had arrived.

'And now this,' Danny went on. 'Well done, Charlotte.'

Charlotte smiled broadly.

'You think that your friend Anton is in that container?' Kofi asked.

Danny shrugged. 'Maybe. It's our best bet.'

'So what do we do?' Paul asked.

Danny smiled, crouching down. 'We need a plan.'

The others nodded.

'Let's assume the men in the Mercedes are coming back,' Danny said.

'Yes,' Charlotte agreed.

'We need to be ready for them.'

'With what?' Paul asked.

The noise of the road filled the silence between the four friends. And Danny started thinking. Racking his brain for stories he'd read where someone was held prisoner and his friends released him.

'There are two things,' Danny said eventually, 'that I can think of.'

The other three looked at him.

'One, use bait to get the people who might be keeping Holt in there to come out. Two, cause a distraction.'

'So which?' Paul said.

'Well, we can't use bait. We're not putting anyone in danger,' Danny said, remembering how terrible he had felt when he thought that Charlotte had been taken. 'So we cause a distraction.'

'How?' Charlotte asked. 'A crash or something?'

'No,' Kofi said in a strong voice.

For once the eyes were off Danny.

'We use bait. We use me.'

'No way,' said Danny. 'We can't put you in danger.'

'It is not important,' Kofi interrupted. 'I am the reason your friend is a prisoner. I am the reason you are all here. I must be the one to help. I am the bait.'

No one spoke. Danny couldn't think of a distraction that would persuade Kofi there was another way that would work.

'If I go there they will come for me,' Kofi went on. 'They will not shoot me with so many people here, will they? It would not happen in Ghana. But here?'

Danny realized that Kofi was asking a question. And that he didn't know the answer.

'No,' Danny decided, 'they wouldn't.'

'So let me go down there. Shearer will come. Or someone. Maybe the men in the silver car? I walk there when they open the door to go in. They come to me. I cause them some trouble. You go in.'

'That's good,' Paul said.

Danny nodded. He had to agree. Although he hated the idea of putting any of them in harm's way. But he was worried about Anton too.

Who knew how much time Anton had? How much danger he was in?

'Or,' Charlotte broke into his thoughts, 'we could call the police. Or IKEA security.'

Paul nodded to that too.

'What if we're wrong?' Danny asked.

'Then we're wrong,' Charlotte went on. 'They're not going to arrest us, are they?' As she said this she smiled at Danny.

'They could do us for wasting police time,' Paul countered.

Charlotte nodded. 'But would they?' she said.

Then something changed. The silver Mercedes was moving slowly through the car park, like the top of a submarine, cutting through the waves.

'There is no time,' Kofi said. 'I will go.' And he darted away.

The three friends left in the shadow of the white van could only watch as he ran among the cars.

Kofi had made the decision for them. He was the bait. And Anton was the prize.

MAN DOWN

Danny, Charlotte and Paul hid behind a lime-green VW camper van two parking bays away from the first of the containers. The containers that Charlotte said might contain Anton Holt.

Kofi was standing among the cars, waiting for the silver Mercedes, hoping it would do another circuit of the car park.

And it did.

The men inside *had* to be something to do with Holt's disappearance.

Eventually the Mercedes stopped in a parking bay fifty metres from the containers. The men got out and one of them approached. He was tall and muscular with dark curly hair. He had his hand on his jacket. As though, Danny thought, he had a gun under it. As the man came closer to the container, he looked to each side, paused, then took a set of keys out of his pocket.

He was standing in front of the container. Unlocking it.

It was time for the next stage of the plan.

Danny turned to see Kofi emerge from among

the cars. The Ghanaian walked quickly towards the containers. Then he slowed down and stood still.

Waiting to be seen.

He's not bothered about his safety at all, Danny thought. *He's just going there saying, Come and get me.* Danny could feel his heart hammering inside his chest.

The curly-haired man had the container padlock open by the time Kofi was standing behind him. At the same moment the second Mercedes man – tall and well built – leapt out of his car and ran towards his colleague. He was shouting. He had seen Kofi.

'Bjorn! Bjorn! Behind you! The boy!'

The first man dropped the padlock and turned to see Kofi now running away.

Danny watched in horror as the two men pursued Kofi around a convertible Porsche Carrera. But he was so fast, so nimble, that they couldn't get near him. Even when the smaller man walked through the car, across the exposed seats, to try to reach him.

This is terrifying, Danny thought. But it was still working like clockwork. Kofi had completely distracted the two men. And now the container was unlocked.

Danny stood up and – with Charlotte and Paul – rushed towards it.

Danny fumbled with a giant lever, then Charlotte and Paul hauled the door open.

It made a horrific noise. On its hinges. A screeching-grinding.

Danny looked in. Paul and Charlotte were at his shoulders.

And there he was. Anton Holt. Squinting like a creature that had never seen daylight.

The three of them rushed towards him. Into the echoing container. Round a stack of pallets that half concealed the journalist. The plan was going to work.

Holt was not tied up, as they had thought he might be, so they just had to lift him to his feet.

Then they turned to drag him to freedom.

And that was when the plan *stopped* going like clockwork.

First Danny heard a shot.

Then a cry of pain and the sound of someone hitting the ground.

In the background there were screams and shouts as other people in the car park ran, terrified.

Then the container door closed.

And they could see nothing, as the noise of the door being shut echoed inside the container. That terrible screeching.

For a moment nobody said anything. They

listened to a rattling sound that they knew was the padlock being put back on. And locked.

There was nothing they could do.

Then Holt spoke in a quiet voice. 'How did they catch you?'

'What?' Danny asked.

'They brought you here. They must have caught you. How did they manage it?' Holt went on.

Neither Charlotte nor Paul had spoken yet.

'Charlotte? Paul?' Danny called, hoping neither of them would answer. He wasn't 100 per cent sure they were in the container.

But they both replied. Together.

'Are you OK?' Holt said, sounding confused.

Holt obviously thought they'd been brought here, so Danny decided to explain. 'We were breaking in to release *you*,' he said. But that was all he could manage. Because a cold feeling had washed over him, like he was caught in a current that was dragging him to the bottom of a deep, wide river.

The three of them – *and* Anton – were locked inside.

One person knew where they were.

And that person, Danny was pretty sure, had just been shot.

THE END

'What happened to Kofi? Did you see?'

Charlotte was the first to speak.

Still no one answered for a minute. No one wanted to.

'I saw him fall,' Paul ventured, his voice dry and slow. 'Before the door shut. After the gunshot.'

Danny nodded. But he realized it was pointless to nod. It was like nodding at his dad. He wondered if this was how his dad felt. In pitch blackness. Confined.

'That's what it sounded like to me too,' Danny said, breaking the latest silence.

Holt spoke next. 'What happened out there?'

Danny gathered his thoughts. What *had* happened? They had come into the container, thinking they could rescue Holt, thinking that Kofi had distracted the two men.

Then the door had closed.

After Kofi had been shot.

It seemed unreal to Danny. How could these things have happened? How could he be trapped in a container with the distinct possibility that he would never get out alive?

Then he realized. His phone. They could just phone someone. He checked the screen.

No network coverage.

Danny's heart sank.

And then the panic started.

In his arms. Followed by a tightness running up his biceps to his shoulders. Then across his chest. He knew it was panic. He knew he had to keep control. He felt a pressure in his head, like it was swelling hugely. He heard voices. Paul and Charlotte, talking to Holt. But he was too under the influence of his body to hear properly. He stood up. His legs had gone wobbly. He wanted to know that he could still use them.

His head was buzzing now. He could see tiny lights swirling in the darkness. He wondered if he was about to faint.

No. He had to keep control. He had to find a way out of this. He had to be strong.

'Danny?'

He heard Charlotte's voice. All fuzzy, making weird echoing sounds. He tried to home in on it. Use it as a focus.

Focus. That was it. He dug his fingernails into his arms.

'Danny?' Charlotte's voice was clearer now.

'Yeah?' he said.

'I asked if you were OK.'

'I'm fine.'

'Then why didn't you answer me?'

Danny could hear an edge in Charlotte's voice. Something he'd not heard before. Maybe it was panic in her too. He could also – somehow – hear the sound of Paul and Holt listening.

'I was trying to think of a way out of this,' Danny said. 'There is a way out of everything.'

There was another long pause. Danny tried to control his thoughts during the silence in the dark. They needed to get out of this rut. Think ahead. Think like real detectives.

He turned his head to where he thought Anton might be.

'What about you, Anton? What's happened to you since they put you here?'

'Nothing.'

Suddenly Anton's face lit up. A great glow around him.

'What's that?' Paul asked.

'My watch,' Anton said. 'It lights up. Quite powerfully.'

'Our phones!' Charlotte shouted.

'What?' Paul said. Then, 'Of course!'

'No reception,' Anton cut in. 'Not on my network.'

'Nor mine,' Danny said reluctantly.

He listened to Charlotte and Paul going into their pockets, saw their faces light up faintly, then their hopeful expressions turn to frowns.

'Nothing,' Charlotte said.

'Nor me,' Paul said.

Another pause. A tense pause that felt like it had lasted an hour but was actually only a few seconds long.

'I'm sorry,' Danny said. 'It's my fault we're here.'

Nobody replied. And Danny wondered if they all blamed him – his wanting to solve football crimes – for bringing them here. If they all thought that he had led them to a slow, painful death.

HERO

When the shot was fired, Kofi hit the floor. He knew instinctively to do that. Although he'd never heard gunfire before, never even handled a gun, he knew to drop to the floor.

He wasn't sure, but he thought he heard the police sirens even before the gunshot. Or maybe at exactly the same time. Either way, both sounds finally pushed Kofi over the edge. His mind was so confused it was hard to make sense of any of the sounds around him. Everything seemed muffled, as if his ears were failing him.

He had to get out of there.

Kofi watched from between the cars where he was hiding. He could see other shoppers running for cover, or hiding, like him, children clustered around their legs. Children crying loud and long. He caught one man's face. It was trembling with fear.

And it was like looking in a mirror. Because that was just how Kofi felt.

Kofi lifted his head to see where the gunmen were. They were not at the container. They were not running away. He lifted his head some more.

And there they were. Crouched by their car. Hiding like everyone else.

When the police car drew up, Kofi felt the urge to run. Just to get away from this hell. He should have done it before coming here, before he decided to help Danny. He should have been selfish then.

So now he *would* be selfish.

Get away from here.

Avoid the police, who would send him to prison for being in the country without a job. Especially the van filled with police officers that had stopped on the edge of the car park, away from the first police car.

So he turned to go. Back through the car park. To London. He could disappear in London. He didn't know where it was. Except he had seen a road sign, 'London 207 miles', from one of the motorway bridges he'd walked over.

That was a start.

As he walked he felt like he was in a dream. He didn't think for a minute about Danny, about the gunmen, the police. He didn't think, full stop. He just walked. It was the only way he could cope with his fear and anxiety and panic.

No thinking.

No thoughts.

That was the answer to this.

Then he stopped.

There was one thought he could not ignore.

He turned back to see the scene in the car park.

The police were talking to people now. A group of them. And the group included the two gunmen, who were casually leaning on their car, pretending they had nothing to do with the shooting.

Kofi looked at the container. It was still shut. With everyone in it.

And he realized that he just couldn't let this happen.

He would not be able to live with himself.

He turned and walked up to the police van. Each step was almost impossible. He had to fight himself not to run away. Because he knew he was putting himself in their hands now. He would be arrested too, whether they got the two gunmen or not. He knew it.

And then there was his fear. The panic still running through him like the traffic on the motorway a few metres away.

He was about to tell the police that the two men they were talking to were armed and ready to kill.

Anything could happen.

Nobody had spoken for over a minute when the door began to open. And a minute is a long time when you are hopelessly trapped in the dark with no idea of what might happen next.

The light was blinding for all of them this time. And in front of them stood three silhouettes.

What is this? Danny wondered. *Have they come to finish the job?* They'd killed Kofi. Now they had four people trapped in an oversized tin can, it would be so easy to step inside, shut the door and execute every one of them.

Danny braced himself. He didn't have time to talk to the others. But he was going to charge, at least try and save the rest of them, even if it cost him.

He didn't think he was being brave. He just thought he had no other option.

As he charged at the opening door, Danny's eyes adjusted quickly to see two policemen and another figure.

Kofi.

Standing up.

Kofi.

Alive and well.

Danny slowed, then sank to his knees, overcome by his adrenalin.

It was OK.

Everything was going to be OK.

SATURDAY

SATURDAY

READ ALL ABOUT IT

AFRICAN FOOTBALLER SAVES FOUR

By Anton Holt, Chief Sports Writer

In the shadow of the City Stadium, yesterday, one of the most remarkable stories in the history of football began to unfold. And almost ended in disaster.

But that disaster was averted. By a hero. Sixteen-year-old African footballer Kofi Danquah.

It began on Thursday morning.

I was leaving the offices of the newspaper, following a lead for a story concerning the mooted takeover of City FC.

In the underground car park at the newspaper, as I opened the door to my car, a delivery van pulled up. I thought the driver was looking for directions.

Because who would expect to have a white van driven up to them in broad daylight and to be bundled into the van, taken away, gagged and bound?

No one.

But that's what happened.

To me.

In seconds I was in the back of a van. Face down. I was in pain and hardly able to breathe.

When the van came to a halt a few minutes later, I was forced out and into an empty container on the outskirts of town.

And that's where I stayed. Without light. Without food. Without water. And – after the first twenty-four hours – without hope.

I thought I would die there.

But at midday yesterday, after being in pitch darkness for more than twenty-four hours, the container was suddenly flooded with fierce daylight. And it's hard to say what was worse. The pain in my eyes. The fear in my heart.

But overpowering all those feelings was hope.

The door was open.

And three young people came in. Three young people whom I cannot name: to protect their identity. But three young people who came to save me – who are heroes too.

But then, heartbreakingly, we were trapped in together.

There was a gunshot.

We thought we had seen the one person who could save us gunned down before our eyes.

All that was left to find out was if we would die from thirst and hunger in the container – or if our captors would come back to finish us off quickly.

Then the doors opened again.

We expected to be met with a hail of bullets.

But we were met instead by Kofi Danquah, who had put his life at risk to rescue the four of us.

Our hero.

Kofi Danquah is the young Ghanaian footballer this reporter wrote about two days ago. He was abandoned by an unscrupulous unofficial football agent, who cheated him and his family out of thousands, and left him in the UK with nothing.

Nothing but broken dreams.

In the article I named Jonathan Shearer, the agent who brought him here.

It seems Jonathan Shearer wasn't pleased.

It seems Jonathan Shearer had me abducted and wanted to blackmail the *Evening Post* into taking back my claims. To ensure that his name – Jonathan Shearer – did not appear in these pages.

That's Jonathan Shearer.

And this is a photograph of him.

The two gunmen who abducted me and who shot at – and, mercifully, missed – Kofi Danquah have confessed to everything. They are in custody. The city is safe from them.

But Jonathan Shearer is *not* in custody.

He is out there.

If you see Jonathan Shearer do not approach him. He is dangerous. Just call 999 and the police will do the rest.

THE TRUTH

Danny's dad sighed. 'Your friend Anton Holt is getting more and more tabloid every week.'

'How do you mean?' Danny asked, putting the newspaper down.

'His writing style. It's a bit . . . melodramatic.'

Danny shrugged. 'He's just telling a story.'

'Hmmmmm,' Dad said. Then he put his hand on Danny's, holding it there. 'So, who were these kids?'

'Kids?' Danny said, shocked his dad was being so direct. And he immediately wished he'd said something else. He just sounded guilty. Incriminating himself.

He wondered how his dad would handle this. Would he skirt around the issue, try to catch Danny out?

'Was it you?'

'What?' Danny said, his voice pitching high.

'Tell me the truth,' Dad said. 'Was that you?'

Danny felt like he'd been punched in the stomach. His dad was asking him to tell him something. His dad was asking him for the truth. His dad, who had always required truth from Danny as the most important thing. And it was something that Danny had always stuck to.

So what should he say?

Should he protect his dad from the truth, to save him the worry?

Should he lie, to avoid the biggest telling-off of his life? That would, no doubt, involve his mum.

Or should he just tell the truth? Face the consequences? Know that, at least, he had been honest with his dad?

'I was there,' Danny said.

Then he watched his dad put his head in his hands.

'You were in the container?' Dad asked eventually.

Danny stared at his dad. 'Yes.'

Then his dad lifted up his face. Danny could see tears in his eyes. He had not seen his dad cry before, not even when he was blinded. But now his dad's eyes were dripping with tears. Tears down his cheeks. Tears down to his chin.

Danny felt bad. Worse than ever. Worse than when he was locked in the container. Worse than when a Russian billionaire's private army was hunting him down in Moscow. Worse than when he was being led to his death in the City Stadium by Sir Richard Gawthorpe's henchman.

'What am I . . .' his dad started. 'What am I supposed to do about this? I am your father. I am supposed to look after you.'

Danny said nothing. He had no answer. He knew his dad should ban him from doing the things he did, trying to solve crimes. That was the only answer.

'Well?'

'I don't know, Dad.'

Danny knew his answer was rubbish. He had to do better than that. So he steeled himself.

'But I know I need to do this, Dad. I love it. If I have to stop, I'll be . . .' Danny didn't know the words to use.

'Nothing?' Dad suggested.

'What?'

'If you stop doing this, then you'll be nothing? You won't be you? You'll never be yourself?'

Now it was Danny whose eyes were filling up with tears. His dad had got him in one. His dad understood him. Now he felt better than ever. Because his dad loved him enough to understand him.

'Yes,' Danny said.

An hour later Danny was back in the city centre. He had a copy of the *Evening Post* under his arm. And he was walking quickly.

He was taking the newspaper to Kofi. He wanted to put Kofi's mind at rest.

After the events of the day before, Anton had put Kofi up in the city's poshest hotel.

A posh hotel for posh people. And therefore a secure hotel.

Danny imagined that Kofi would be going out of his mind in the hotel. He would be so out of his comfort zone.

Danny hoped that showing Kofi the newspaper would convince him that Jonathan Shearer was long gone. That there was no way he would still be in the city. Or the country.

Danny approached the hotel's reception. There was a proper reception area this time. A long wooden counter. Staff in suits.

'Yes, sir,' a woman behind the counter said.

Danny reeled. She was so good-looking. He could barely bring himself to speak to her.

'Could you call Kofi Danquah, please?' Danny asked. His voice cracked and squeaked.

The woman looked Kofi up on her computer.

'Mr Danquah,' she said in a French accent that made Danny feel weak at the knees. 'I'm sorry. He is gone.'

Danny stared at the woman. 'Gone?'

'Yes, sir. Gone.'

Kofi had run off again.

After a moment, Danny came to his senses. He uttered a 'Thank you' to the lady, then walked quickly out of the hotel. But inside he was feeling terrible. Where the hell was Kofi now? He had no need to run away. He had been safe there.

Danny wanted time on his own. To think. To deal with the terrible feeling he had that things were about to go horribly wrong.

Again.

For everyone.

But he was *not* alone. Because close behind him, wearing a hat and sunglasses, freshly shaven, was Jonathan Shearer, football agent and killer.

KOFI ALONE

Kofi remembered the way he had come. Up the eight-lane highway that led from the city centre, away from the football stadium. It didn't take much imagination to find the airport anyway. He just had to follow the line of planes descending noisily over the warehouses and tower blocks of the city.

And it was good that Kofi didn't need much imagination. Because his mind was frozen. The events of the last few days and the strangeness of this foreign country, of Europe, had left him burnt out.

The hotel that Kofi had stayed in was the most luxurious and grand thing that he had ever seen in his whole life. But Kofi could think *only* of being at the airport.

Somehow, he said to himself, he would get a ticket to fly home. Somehow he would get out of this hellhole. And if he couldn't, then he would live at the airport. He had heard about people actually doing that. At least he would be closer to home – and home was far away from the man who was still looking for him.

So he walked quickly by parades of shops, past hundreds of red-brick houses all packed together on hillsides. So many homes. And as he walked he listened to the sound of every car approaching from behind, in case he heard one of them slowing to stop. And the danger it might bring.

For a while he tried to go down the back streets, to avoid the busy route, but a group of boys had called after him, then chased him, and he had run as fast as he could, faster than any of them could, feeling angry. After that he decided to come back to the main road. It was safer. Probably.

He walked. Trying not to think about all the things that had pushed him to this: to feeling like he couldn't cope any longer, to the panic and the fear.

Arriving here to find no place at City FC for him.

Realizing his dreams were shattered.

Meeting Danny, talking to the journalist. The hope he had foolishly felt.

Then running from Shearer, once Danny had had the call.

Then the crazy day when guns had been fired and Danny and his friends had been locked in that container.

He wanted to get away from this country.

Fast.

Kofi kept listening to the sound of the traffic,

kept waiting for a car to slow. But all the cars were rushing past him. Unaware of his life. Unaware of him. He was just a boy walking somewhere.

Now he was further out of town the houses were bigger, set back from the road. They had gardens with grass and small trees. There were lights on in windows. He wondered how many people lived in each house. They were huge and looked lavish.

And then he heard a car slowing. He recognized the shifting down of gears, the different sound the car was making from the others.

He was not mistaken.

Should he look back? Or just go on walking? Or run down a side street and risk being caught by one of those gangs again?

He decided to look back.

His heart jumped.

A police car. A small white car with 'Police' written on the side and bonnet.

What now? They might check his papers and realize he was not meant to be here – he was still meant to be in the hotel room where Anton had put him. He might be taken away. Somewhere. He didn't know where. He didn't know how the police worked in this strange country.

Kofi watched the policewoman in the passenger seat eye him. And he decided to wave, like he had to the football stadium guard on his first day here. To be friendly, not guilty. He might as well try.

He was happy to see the woman smile back, then the police car accelerate away, lost in the stream of never-ending traffic.

Kofi breathed out. It was OK. Everything was going to be OK.

A kilometre later, Kofi saw the turn-off for the airport and followed the signs. He didn't have a clue what he was going to do when he got there, but that was where he wanted to be.

CITY SEARCH

Danny knew he had to use his brain before he began his search for Kofi. He could just go looking everywhere he could think of, through the streets, feeling more and more anxious. Or he could sit down and come up with a plan.

Where could Kofi be? Where did he actually know in the city?

But they weren't the most important questions. The most important question was: why would Kofi have run off? And, if Danny could work out what had motivated him to run off, that would help him to answer the other questions.

He knew he had got this technique from a detective novel. The kind that wasn't all about shooting guns, with a dead body on every other page. The novel Danny was thinking of had a detective who sat down and made notes in a book every time he found some new piece of evidence or a clue. He would sit and think about what his suspect would be thinking, why and how he had come round to it.

So Danny went to City Square, the very centre

of town, and tried to think like Kofi. He sat in the shadow of the statue there, a huge iron man on a huge iron horse.

Why had Kofi run away?

Fear. It had to be fear.

But what was he afraid of?

Shearer?

Maybe.

Although Danny thought Shearer might have left the country by now.

The gunmen?

Definitely.

He was in a strange country and having men shoot at him must have been terrifying. Danny tried to think how he would feel if he was in Ghana suddenly and someone had shot at him – and might do it again.

Yes, it was definitely fear that had sent Kofi into hiding.

Danny shuffled on the base of the statue. Its cold hard stone had frozen his bottom.

Danny wondered where he would go if he was scared and in a strange place.

Somewhere he knew. That's what Danny was sure of.

So where did Kofi know?

The industrial estate.

IKEA.

The two hotels he had stayed in.

The newspaper offices he must have seen from opposite his first hotel.

Was that all?

Danny thought so.

So he had five places to look.

So what should he do? Just go to those places, straight up to them?

No.

One, there was a chance that Kofi did not want Danny to find him. He was scared. His mind might be so disturbed that he could be thinking anything of Danny.

Two, Danny didn't want to rule out the fact that Jonathan Shearer might still be in the UK – and looking for Kofi. It was a long shot. But possible. So Danny couldn't rule it out.

Danny decided he would approach all five places from the back, or at least not from the front. You never knew who might be looking.

He made a list of all the places he needed to go – and the order in which he could do them the quickest.

The second hotel Kofi had stayed in, the posh one.

IKEA.

The industrial estate.

The newspaper offices.

The first hotel.

Danny checked his watch. He still had hours before he needed to go home. He was fine.

Then he set off. Round the back way.

To the posh hotel.

IKEA.

The industrial estate.

The newspaper offices.

But there was no sign of Kofi at any of them. Nothing. And now that there was only one possibility left, Danny was seriously starting to doubt his strategy. He was running out of time.

This was his last chance.

He would approach the other hotel through the bushes that surrounded its car park by the inner ring road. You could get in around the back of one of the bus stops. Have a look to see if Kofi was anywhere there.

Five minutes later, Danny was squatting in the bushes round the back of the hotel. It was one of those cheap hotels that had no fancy reception area or restaurant. Just a front desk and dozens of adequate rooms.

Danny watched a half-naked man with a fat

stomach lounging back on his bed, the TV screen flickering colours back on his skin.

Then another man in the next room tapping away on a keyboard, talking to himself.

Danny was so engrossed he didn't hear the sound of footsteps approaching.

The first thing he knew was when his view of the two men in their adjacent rooms was broken by the shape of a handgun.

Looking back, Danny would swear that his heart stopped at that moment.

'Get out.' A deep South African-sounding voice barked at Danny. 'Out! Now!'

Danny looked at the gun. His legs had gone to jelly and he couldn't stand. But he also knew he had to. This was a man with a weapon.

He tried to speak, but no words would come.

Then he saw the gun raised and pointed in his direction.

'You must be Danny.' There was no mistaking that voice. It was Jonathan Shearer.

THE END OF THE ROAD

Danny often wondered about the films and books in which people are held at gunpoint.

Whenever someone had a gun pointed at someone else, the *someone else* would immediately do everything that the gunman – or woman – wanted them to. It was like that child's game: Simon-says. You have the gun, therefore you can say exactly what everyone else has to do.

Danny had often run through this scenario in his mind: having a gun pointed at him like this. It had happened before. More than once.

This time, faced with Jonathan Shearer, he really wanted to stand up and say, 'Put the gun away.' But then, if he did say that, he might get shot. They were hidden away at the back of a car park. A noisy road nearby. Maybe a gun's shot would go unnoticed.

Danny decided not to risk it.

He put his hands over his head – like they always did in films – and he moved out of the bushes.

'You are the boy who has Kofi Danquah's mobile

phone, yes?' Shearer asked, pushing the gun at Danny.

Danny nodded. It was all he could do to keep himself upright, let alone speak.

'And where is Kofi Danquah?'

Danny shrugged. He knew he would have to speak soon, or this man with his gun might become irritated. It was just the fear he was feeling was utterly overwhelming.

'I'm looking for him too,' Danny said.

'Hmmmm,' Shearer said. 'I think if I have you he might come to me. Do you?'

Danny shook his head. He wasn't sure what the man meant.

'I do,' Shearer went on.

'He doesn't know where I am. Like I don't know where he is,' Danny said, glancing at the gun that was still pressing against his chest.

And then they were both suddenly distracted by oncoming lights.

Danny realized what was happening first and, knowing it was a car coming in through the entrance to the hotel car park, he lunged at Shearer. And because Shearer had been standing at an unusual angle to point the gun at Danny, he fell. Backwards. Danny saw him sprawl on the floor. And then, because he knew he had to put him out of action for a few seconds at least, Danny kicked him. In the balls. Hard.

He heard Shearer groan and then start coughing. Danny had bought himself some time.

So he ran away. Quickly.

Danny didn't look back to check what Shearer was doing. He just ran. He wanted to get to Kofi as soon as he could, wherever he was. And he definitely wanted to get away from this man.

The best escape route was up the hill that led away from the City Stadium.

So he went for it.

But not along the road. That was too obvious. And if Shearer had a car he'd be able to pick him off, do a drive-by shooting, if he really meant what he had said.

So Danny ran in the fields that ran parallel to the road. Fields bordered by more bushes.

Perfect. Especially as Danny was wearing black. He always wore black. In case he needed to go undercover. It was his habit now.

He ran.

Over a stile.

Into the fields.

Among the shadows.

At first he thought he was OK. At first he thought he had got away.

But then – just as a jumbo jet came roaring over his head – he saw the fence post ahead of him disintegrate. A bullet had shattered it.

He thought he was running fast until that happened. But somehow he managed to double his speed.

He knew Shearer was behind him.

He knew he was firing bullets.

And he knew he had a good chance of dying in this field.

He didn't need to look back to see that. All he had to do was run. Not think – just run.

But, as he did, a strange memory came into his head, of racing through the soft grass up the steep hill. His dad. Teaching him how to run. Don't look back at the people behind you: they'll drag you back. Look at the people ahead of you: they'll pull you forward.

So when he reached a stile he didn't look back to check how far behind Shearer was. Instead he pulled himself over the stile. Then he ran again, in a slight zigzag in case he was still being shot at. Moving into the trees for a few seconds when he could. Hoping Shearer would think he had disappeared into the impenetrable woods.

But no more bullets came. Even when another giant plane came hurtling out of the sky. So this time, when Danny reached the top of the hill and leapt over a drystone wall, he took a look.

Shearer was well out of range. He had even given up the chase and was staggering back towards the road, where the silver Mercedes was waiting. Heading up the hill too.

And in that minute – Danny knew where Kofi would be.

At the airport.

Where he had arrived.

Where he had arrived in England before his life had gone so disastrously wrong.

The problem was that Danny was pretty sure that's where Shearer would be headed too. And he'd be getting there a good half an hour before Danny.

Danny would just have to keep going.

AIRPORT

Kofi was not sure why he was at the airport. It was just where he felt best.

One, it was warm.

Two, it was as near to home as he could ever be now.

Home.

Ghana.

Two words he'd barely thought about for days, but that were now like mantras to him. Comforting. Like a hug from his mother.

A part of him knew that being here would do no good. That he had no plane ticket. That, if he found one on the floor, he would not be able to jump on a plane back to Accra. But just being near the planes was better than being in that hotel. With its long corridors and people passing you silently, casting their eyes down, unsmiling. Better than freezing in an abandoned building.

At least he would be among all the people and security men – and safe from Jonathan Shearer.

Danny got the bus to the airport. He had thought

about running, but just as he came out of the field there was a bus stop, with a double-decker pulled up heading for the airport.

So he got on it.

It made sense. He needed to conserve his energy. He needed time to think.

He had ten minutes on the bus. He sat on the top deck. Alone. The bottom deck was packed with people guarding huge suitcases and bags.

Danny used the time to work out a plan.

One, locate Kofi.

Two, avoid Shearer.

That was it. That was what he had to achieve.

It sounded simple, but Danny knew that simple was the last thing it would be.

There was a grey beanie hat on the bus. Someone had left it on a seat. Danny decided it would make a good disguise. From Shearer. So he put it on, pulling it over his ears. He'd hand it back to the bus company after he'd done what he needed to do.

As the bus approached the airport, Danny stood up and went down to the lower deck, so he could be first off the bus. If he waited he'd be behind a hundred suitcases on wheels. And one thing he didn't have was time.

Danny recognized the glass front and great steel tubes of City Airport. Where he used to come on his birthday when he was younger, when he was obsessed with planes.

He and his dad would sit in one of the cafés and watch them taking off and landing. He loved seeing them in the rain most of all, jumbo jets leaving a great trail of spray behind them.

Then Charlotte came into Danny's mind. And Paul. And he realized he'd missed a third element out of his plan: backup.

So he took his last minute on the bus to text Paul and Charlotte:

Help. Meet me at airport. But be careful.
Shearer around. D

The airport's sliding doors opened to welcome him when he arrived. Danny had decided *not* to rush into the airport. He walked with the first few people who had got off his bus. To be part of a crowd with bags. Not a lone boy at an airport, without bags.

Once inside the glass doors, Danny set about finding Kofi.

He used all the techniques he could remember from reading about detectives tracking people.

One, wear some sort of casual disguise. He had that covered: his new hat.

Two, blend into the crowd. Walk with other groups of people, never on your own, or you'll stand out.

And, three, behave like a normal airport user would behave. Don't act in a way that makes you look like you're not there to either catch a plane or meet someone off a plane. Wander round shops. Sit in cafés. Stand in queues.

Danny worked his way up the airport concourse. He couldn't go through security to be airside, so he focused on the main shopping and café areas. He decided to be as thorough as he could be.

The first thing that struck him was how uncluttered the walls of the airport were. Just white wall after white wall, very little else. It would be hard to hide in an airport. It looked to Danny like it had been designed to stop people concealing things. Like bombs, he imagined.

He also noticed how many locked doors there were along the walls of the airport. Doors that occasionally security or airport staff would disappear into. He smiled when he saw that one airport worker, his sleeves rolled up, had a huge City FC tattoo on his forearm. Danny watched him go to the door, key in a security code and disappear behind the great white wall.

C4284Z.

Danny tried to think of a way of remembering the security code. His dad's age: 42. Then his dad's age doubled: 84. That would do it: 4284.

It took Danny just ten minutes to search the entire area. But there was no sign of Kofi. And he'd been very systematic, making sure he missed nothing.

Maybe he was wrong, he thought. Maybe Kofi and Shearer were somewhere else, having their showdown. They could be anywhere in the city. Shearer might already have caught up with Kofi.

The thought chilled him.

But Danny decided not to be rash and head off somewhere else. He would go and have a drink in one of the airport cafés. He could watch from there, hidden behind the sports pages. Something might still happen.

Mindful of needing to keep a low profile, he walked casually up to the café. Behind a family of three. A mum, dad and a daughter. Danny could easily have been their son. It was a good cover.

But just before they reached the café the family veered off to go to the toilet. And Danny was exposed. Seriously exposed. Because there, in the café, with one of his henchmen, was Jonathan Shearer. But Shearer didn't see Danny at all. In fact, he seemed to be watching something in the distance, his body poised now, lifting off his chair.

Danny looked at what Shearer was eyeing. He knew what it would be. Or *who* it would be.

Kofi.

Kofi moving sluggishly, his eyes fixed on the ground.

Kofi. About as vulnerable as he could be.

Danny acted first. Anticipating Shearer's next move would be quick too, he sprinted at Kofi. Silently and then, when Kofi caught his eye, shouting, 'Run.'

Kofi appeared to wake up suddenly and set off towards the far end of the airport concourse. Danny noticed people stop to watch the two of them running.

And, looking round, he saw Shearer and another of his cronies walking rapidly after them.

Gradually, as they ran away from the cafés and shops, the concourse became quieter. There were no check-in desks here. No need for people to come this far. It was only for staff.

And Danny knew there was nowhere to hide. The walls so white, no hiding places, apart from the locked security doors he'd seen workers going in and out of.

What could he do now?

He looked back. The two men were closing in on them, the crony with his hand inside his jacket.

But then it came to him. That was it. The doors. Danny was running alongside Kofi now.

'The door at the end,' Danny panted. 'I know the code.'

'Who are they?' Kofi shouted, casting his eyes back to Shearer.

Danny knew Kofi knew. That he simply didn't want to hear it. But Danny wanted him to understand just how dangerous a situation they were in.

'It's Shearer,' Danny said, spelling it out. 'And he's armed.'

They reached the security door as Danny said this. Kofi seemed to lose all his energy. Fear had overcome him.

Danny lunged at the door and tapped in the code: C4284Z.

He pushed the door, casting his eyes back to Shearer and his henchman. They were fifty metres away, slowing down, thinking they had Danny and Kofi now.

But the door wouldn't open. Danny twisted at the knob. It wouldn't budge.

Shearer was twenty metres away now. Danny could see his grin. A vicious, murderous grin.

And Danny could feel panic overwhelming him. This had to work. This last attempt at opening the door.

They were both dead otherwise.

So Danny tried to take control. Tried to get a grip of his trembling hands.

C4284Z.

He twisted the knob again. And it worked!

Danny grabbed Kofi and pulled him through the door.

Away from Shearer.

His loud and terrifying voice.

His violent banging on the door.

And straight into the arms of the large security guard he'd seen minutes earlier.

GOODBYE, SHEARER

'Now then, lads,' the giant security man said, grabbing a boy firmly in each arm, 'how did you manage that?'

As he spoke, the banging on the door grew louder. They could all hear shouting. And the security guard moved to open the door.

'No,' Danny shouted. 'There's a man on the other side of that door who wants to kill us. He's armed.'

'Come on, lads,' the security man said. 'Do you expect me to believe that?'

Danny needed inspiration. He had to convince the man not to open the door.

'I swear on your City tattoo,' he blurted out, 'I'm not lying.'

The security guard glanced at his tattoo. Then at Danny.

'What?'

More banging. The sound of a shoulder against the door.

'Please. You've got to believe us.' It was Kofi speaking now. 'I am the boy who came over to play for City, but . . .'

'The Ghanaian lad?' The man looked interested now.

'Yes,' Kofi said.

'So the guy on the other side of the door is that agent? The one I read about in the paper?'

'Yes,' Danny said.

'Right. You two in that room. Stay there.' The man pointed to another doorway. 'I'll sort this one.'

Danny and Kofi rushed into the room and closed the door as the security guard walked towards the main security door.

The two boys listened as he opened the door.

'Yes, gentlemen?'

'Those two boys.' It was Shearer's frightening voice. 'Where are they?'

'What boys? There's just me in here. On my break.'

'I want them.'

Shearer's voice was loud. Danny could see it scared the hell out of Kofi.

'Maybe you'd like to talk to these guys about it,' the security guard said.

Danny and Kofi risked having a look at what was happening in the corridor. They could just about see behind Shearer through the door.

A group of six men were standing behind Shearer

and his partner, with machine guns pointing at them.

'They're the airport's rapid armed response unit,' the guard said. 'And you are going to get what's coming to you.'

They watched Shearer and his crony raise their hands.

'You gonna put that gun down?' the guard said. 'Or am I going to have to take it off you?'

The crony handed the gun over. Meekly.

He and Shearer were under arrest.

When Danny looked at Kofi's face at that moment, the picture of relief and happiness was amazing to see. And Danny knew he'd done something good.

Three hours later, Danny walked with Kofi out of the airport. Charlotte and Paul were sitting in the café near the door. They came over. Kofi hugged each of them. Danny could see he was nearly in tears. He felt that way himself.

As Kofi was talking to Paul, Charlotte handed Danny the final edition of the day's *Evening Post*.

'Look at this,' she said, leaning into him.

Danny looked at the article, then beamed a broad smile.

'Tell him,' he said to Charlotte.

Charlotte shook her head. 'No, you tell him.'

Danny watched Charlotte draw Paul aside. Now Danny was walking with Kofi.

'There's something else I have to tell you,' Danny said to Kofi.

Kofi looked at him, his face wary, the smile gone.

'No, it's good,' Danny said.

Kofi smiled. 'What?'

Danny opened the newspaper in front of him.

CITY TO OFFER GHANA HERO A TRIAL

Then Kofi did start crying. Tears of joy. Tears that meant this whole ordeal was over – and that there was hope he could repay his family in a way he'd thought was gone forever.

TWO WEEKS LATER

HERO'S RETURN

The pick-up truck bounced along the road, hitting potholes, pushing Danny and Kofi against each other as they headed out of the city. All the windows were open. It was baking hot. And the air coming in through the window wasn't making it any cooler.

Kofi's mother's cousin Raphael was sitting at the front, driving.

Danny had been so happy to see Kofi and Raphael reunited at the arrivals hall in Accra airport. They had thrown their arms around each other and talked and talked. It made Danny feel good that he had played a small part in making this reunion happen.

Kofi looked at Danny. 'You OK?'

Danny nodded. 'Hot,' he yelped as they hit another pothole.

Kofi shrugged, then shook his head, grinning.

They had been sitting in silence as Danny stared out of the window at Ghana. First the drive through the city. Hundreds of people on the streets, some coming up to the windows to try to sell things to him. Or to beg.

Danny had been tired after the flights. First from home to Accra, capital of Ghana. Then on a small propeller plane to Kumasi. But now his senses were alive with the adrenalin of being in a new place.

The pick-up left the city and headed along orange-earth roads. Enormous plants and trees grew on either side. People walked slowly, some carrying piles of wood, some with children and one man with what looked like a large dead squirrel that he was offering for sale.

Danny had never been to Africa before. He had been nervous about what he would see. He knew Ghana would be very different from home. The thing that caught him most was the smell. Not a bad smell. Just a different smell. A smell of vegetation and heat and humidity.

He turned to look at his friend.

Kofi was now a City FC player. He had a full contract for two years. His trial had gone extremely well. And City had asked to sign him on the day. They helped him find a reputable agent and – after talking to his family on the phone – Kofi had agreed to be a City player.

Now he was coming home.

Not in a posh car or a private plane.

But certainly with some money. Money for his family.

'Raphael has told me some news about my family,' Kofi said as they neared his home village.

Danny nodded, eager to hear, hoping it would be more good news for them.

'They have a new cocoa farm. From my uncle, who has split his farm in two to help them.'

'Good,' said Danny.

'And now they are no longer cheated. They do not take their cocoa to the old buyer. Now they are part of a group of farmers called Kuapa Kokoo.'

'Is that good?'

'Yes. Now they own their farm and are part of a cooperative, a group of farms. My brothers go to a school paid for by the cocoa. They even own the company that makes the chocolate. So no one can come and take all the profits away from the farmers.'

'Brilliant,' Danny said.

Danny stepped back when they arrived at Kofi's village. Not only did his mother and father come out to greet him. But the whole village, led by a stream of children in blue school uniforms, beaming smiles.

The village was a series of shacks either side of the main road. Some were plastered, but many were made of mud bricks. Every building had a corrugated-iron roof. No tiles. The streets were not covered in tarmac; they were just earth packed hard. And around the feet of children and adults there were small herds of goats, searching for any spare vegetation.

Danny meant to stay out of the celebrations. To give Kofi a chance to see everyone.

But the thing was, everyone wanted to talk to him too.

'*Obroni! Obroni!*' the younger children shouted.

'What does it mean?' Danny asked Kofi as they sat to eat.

'White man,' he replied. 'Some of them will have barely ever seen white people before.'

Danny grinned. And he had to admit to himself that it felt odd. All day, since leaving the airport in Kumasi, he'd seen no other white people. Not from the pick-up. Nor here.

For the first time in his life he felt very white.

Later, as Danny was watching Kofi going round giving gifts to adults in the village, his mobile phone rang. The screen said 'unknown number', but he was so surprised to be getting a call in the middle of nowhere that he answered. It would be good to hear someone from home.

'Hello?'

'It's me,' a voice said. 'Charlotte.'

'Hi. How are you?'

'I'm fine. But more importantly, how are you? How's Ghana?'

'Great.'

'I wanted to call you with some news,' Charlotte said.

'Yeah?' Suddenly Danny felt worried: Charlotte sounded anxious.

'The City buyout. It looks like it's going ahead. They reckon it's Russians. But it could be Americans.'

Danny frowned. That *was* bad news. The worst news. Now City would belong to some remote group of people who had never even seen the team play.

'I'm sorry,' Charlotte said.

After the call Danny couldn't stop thinking about City. Even though he was in a part of the world that was very different from his own.

He looked around at the farmers. They'd think he was mad worrying about something like that.

But then something came into his mind. The farmers. How they all owned the company that made the chocolate. How it was called fair trade because all the people who made it benefited from it. They could control it, decide what happened.

237

That was it, Danny decided. That was what they needed to do at City.

When he got back he was going to make it happen. If the farmers here could do it, so could he – and 50,000 City fans.

When he got home he was going to do everything to tell people about these farmers, so that they could do the same.

He turned his face up to the sun, feeling the heat of the rays beam down. He just hoped he wasn't too late.

THANK-YOUS

Thanks, first, to Rebecca and Iris for their love and support while I was writing *Off Side*. Also for putting up with my disappearing to Ghana for a week. And to Rebecca in particular for having so many great ideas that made that trip to Ghana and the story much more fruitful. And for reading it in its various stages and spotting my many mistakes and clumsinesses.

Next, thanks to my agent, David Luxton of Luxton Harris Ltd, for the enthusiasm, advice and support, and for being so great. Leeds! Leeds! Leeds!

To Ian Hawkey, the author of the best book on African football by far, *Feet of the Chameleon* (Portico, 2009), which was a perfect grounding, gave me lots of ideas and led to my meeting up with the Right to Dream Football Academy in Ghana.

To Tom Vernon at Right to Dream (*www.righttodream.com*) and to his colleagues Andy and Josh. I spent two days with them, watching football, meeting footballers and talking about football in Africa. It was invaluable and great fun. They were very generous with their time.

To Bismark and Raphael, two Ghanaian boys who gave me lots of time and answered all my questions.

To Divine Chocolate Ltd in the UK (Charlotte, Tom, Sara and Natasha) who set up my trip to the cocoa farms in Ghana, where I learned about fair-trade chocolate and the Kuapa Kokoo farmers cooperative, which owns 45% of Divine. And to Kuapa Kokoo's Development Officers, Erica and Kwabena, who showed me around the farms in central Ghana. And to Charlotte again for reading the book to help me get it as straight as possible.

For more information about fair-trade chocolate, Kuapa Kokoo and Divine Chocolate Ltd, visit *www.divinechocolate.com* and *www.papapaa.org*. Or take action and sign up as a Dubble Agent at *www.dubble.co.uk* and join thousands of young fair-trade sleuthers on a mission to get fair play for cocoa farmers in Ghana!

To Naomi Danquah, who gave me ideas and leads that made researching the novel far easier than it would have been otherwise, and who kindly read the manuscript to check for problems.

To Ralph Newbrook and Jim Sells for ideas, contacts and encouragement along the way.

Thank you to my writing group in Leeds: Rachel

Connor, Sophie Hannah and James Nash. Their reading of my drafts is always extremely helpful and improves the books immeasurably.

Thanks too to Tony Yeboah (Leeds United, 1995–7) for the goal that inspired the one early in this book.

Thank you, finally, to Puffin. Everyone at the publishers works so hard to make the books as good as they can be and to ensure they reach lots of people. They are the best and no one at Puffin deserves more thanks than my editor, Lindsey Heaven, who not only edits the books (a task in itself) but champions them too. Thanks, Lindsey.

There are some excellent websites about football and its highs and lows. If you want to know more about the darker – or brighter – side of the game, I recommend *www.footballshiddenstory.com*, *www.playthegame*.org, *www.soccerlens.com* and *www.bbc.co.uk/football*.

Three great books about West Africa and its relationship with Europe are *I am Justice: A Journey Out of Africa* by Paul Kenyon (Preface, 2009), *Black Gold of the Sun: Searching for Home in England and Africa* by Ekow Eshun (Penguin, 2006) and *The Belly of the Atlantic* by Fatou Diome (which is also about football!) (Serpent's Tail, 2006). All were very useful. As was Jonas

Scherrens's online dissertation, *The Muscle Drain of African Football Players to Europe*. But, as I said, the best book on African football is *Feet of the Chameleon: The Story of African Football* by Ian Hawkey.

TOM PALMER Q&A

Why did you set *Off Side* in Ghana?

I'd read about young African footballers being cheated by agents. A lot of them come from Ghana or the Ivory Coast. When I'm writing a book I need to go to the place where it is set, to get my facts right. And they speak English in Ghana.

So you went to Ghana?

Yes. I was shown around football academies; my guide was Manchester United's chief scout for Africa. I also got to see a real cocoa farm, where they grow the beans for fair-trade chocolate.

Did you meet any players?

Yes, some of the Ghana under-twenties squad and some youth players who are destined for Man U. I also went to Tony Yeboah's house. He used to play for Leeds. But he was out.

What's Ghana like?

Great. The people are nice. Lots of fun. The best bit was when I went to talk in a school there and they asked me to sing English football songs. So I gave them lots of Leeds songs at full blast. The whole school came to watch me.

Which other countries would you like to set books in?

I'm planning to set a Foul Play book in Italy. I like pizza, coffee and wine. All at their best in Italy. And the football's not bad too.

Ten things you (possibly) didn't know about TOM PALMER

Tom was possibly left as newborn in a box at the door of an adoption home in 1967.

He has got an adopted dad and a step-dad, but has never met his real dad.

Tom's best job – before being an author – was a milkman. He delivered milk for nine years.

He once scored two goals direct from the corner flag in the same game. It was very windy.

Tom did not read a book by himself until he was seventeen.

In 1990 Tom wrecked his knee while playing for Bulmershe College in Reading. He didn't warm up and has regretted it ever since.

He was the UK's 1997 Bookseller of the Year.

He met his wife in the Sahara Desert.

Tom has been to watch over 500 Leeds United games, with Leeds winning 307. He once went for twenty-one years without missing a home game. His wife has been ten times, with Leeds winning every time.

Tom once met George Best in a London pub. Tom wanted to borrow his newspaper to find out the football scores. George kindly obliged.

Ten REAL football crimes

1. In the mid-1990s several English Premiership evening games had to be postponed mid-game because betting syndicates tampered with the floodlights, switching the lights off.

2. In 1966 the World Cup trophy was stolen from a window in Birmingham, where it was being displayed to promote the World Cup finals. It was found later by a dog.

3. Several Liverpool players have been burgled in the last few years while they played away in Europe. Most notably, Steven Gerrard's wide was confronted by four masked men in 2007.

4. Former Everton and West Ham star Mark Ward was jailed for renting a house that was used to store £1 million's worth of illegal drugs.

5. In 2007 a friend of German football supremo Franz Beckenbauer was shot dead in South Africa as the country prepared for the World Cup preliminary draw. On the same day the German team manager had his briefcase stolen.

6. In 2007 Newcastle midfielder Joey Barton was jailed for 74 days for having a fight outside a Liverpool nightclub.

7. In 1994 the Columbian defender Andres Escobar was shot dead, following his scoring of a notorious own goal in the 1994 World Cup finals. Many think it was because drug barons lost a lot of money because of the goal.

8. In 2008 another Colombian player shot dead a fan who'd heckled him about how badly he had been playing. He was jailed.

9. In 1970 Bobby Moore, the England captain, was arrested in Colombia and charged with stealing jewellery. He was quickly released, once it became clear he had been set up.

10. In 2007 the former Manchester City keeper Ashley Timms admitted to trying to blackmail a Premier League footballer, claiming he had an interesting video of him.

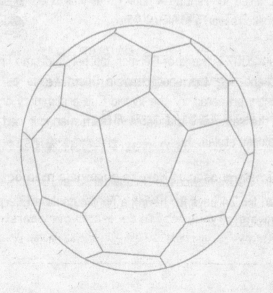

It all started with a Scarecrow.

Puffin is seventy years old.

Sounds ancient, doesn't it? But Puffin has never been
so lively. We're always on the lookout for the next big
idea, which is how it began all those years ago.

Penguin Books was a big idea from the mind of
a man called Allen Lane, who in 1935 invented
the quality paperback and changed the world.
**And from great Penguins, great Puffins grew,
changing the face of children's books forever.**

The first four Puffin Picture Books were hatched in 1940 and the
first Puffin story book featured a man with broomstick arms called
Worzel Gummidge. In 1967 Kaye Webb, Puffin Editor, started the
Puffin Club, promising to **'make children into readers'**.
She kept that promise and over 200,000 children became
devoted Puffineers through their quarterly instalments of
Puffin Post, which is now back for a new generation.

Many years from now, we hope you'll look back and
remember Puffin with a smile. **No matter what your age
or what you're into, there's a Puffin for everyone.**
The possibilities are endless, but one thing is for sure:
whether it's a picture book or a paperback, a sticker book
or a hardback, **if it's got that little Puffin
on it – it's bound to be good.**